J. M. Ava is a European woman who lives in London. She has a broad range of interests, such as world literature, history and arts, which has fuelled her vivid imagination. She has been a muse for a poet whose book was published abroad and has influenced her for her writing.

J. M. Ava had danced classical ballet from a very early age, which has laid a foundation for appreciating the finer things in life.

Her life has been full of colourful experiences, some of them beyond imagination, which have become a source of inspiration for her stories.

Through her charitable works, she has met people from all walks of life. Thus she has understood the lives of unfortunate people and has deepened her perception of the full colours of life.

Her stories are an inspiration for everyone who loves fantasy and fairy tales.

For my mother, who is the most caring person and my closest friend, who has always been there for me and has been inspiring me with her unconditional love.

J. M. Ava

Crystal Pieces of Fantasy

Illustrations by Emma Ungureanu

AUSTIN MACAULEY PUBLISHERS™
LONDON · CAMBRIDGE · NEW YORK · SHARJAH

A CIP catalogue record for this title is available from the British Library.

ISBN 9781528907033 (Paperback)
ISBN 9781528907040 (Hardback)
ISBN 9781528958479 (ePub e-book)

www.austinmacauley.com

First Published (2019)
Austin Macauley Publishers Ltd
25 Canada Square
Canary Wharf
London
E14 5LQ

Contents

The Herbalist

Delaida barely walked, weakened by the hunter's poison arrow. She has been agonising for several days, since the arrow scratched her skin and death started flowing through her veins. She was wandering alone through the woods, surrounded by frightening animal sounds, seeking for a way to save herself. He was following her closely for a long time, hot on her heels. One of his arrows left a scratch, the poison penetrated the flesh and was now draining her life out little by little. It was only a matter of time until she fell down breathless.

Delaida was raised in a small house near Lake Bretava. It was in the heart of the mountains, where people founded several small villages that grew over time and merged into a town – Merab. Merab was a thriving city in Delaida's time which was seething with life. People lived calmly, doing their daily activities and enjoying life, which flowed smoothly and endlessly. The whole area was flourishing under the rulers of the Tanassi clan.

But that was about to change.

A rumour was spreading that the merciless invaders from the north, the Haudi tribe, were conquering the surrounding lands. Fear enveloped people's hearts. It was a matter of time for Merab to be taken over by them.

Delaida grew into a tender, beautiful maiden who stood out from the other girls in her own way. She had keen eyes and a sharp mind. Maybe that was the reason why, when the Houdi tribe, the merciless invaders from the north passed through Merab, the Hunter chose her. Delaida was scared when she noticed that a young Houdi man was gazing at her. He wore a hunter's clothes and a quiver of arrows and a bow hung on his back. She was carrying a bucket of water, which she had to bring to her house. The young man, who was twirling a blade of grass between his lips, started walking deliberately towards her. His gait gave out what he was – an unyielding conqueror. Delaida didn't know what to do, if she left that would make the fierce warrior mad, but if she stayed what would he demand of her? She felt weak, as if she was trapped, so she just froze. The conqueror approached her and put his muddy boot on the well. He spat out the blade of grass right in front of Delaida.

"You local girls look good," he started a conversation while studying her with a ferocious look in his eyes.

She felt her hands shaking while holding the heavy bucket of water. At that moment, some girl from the town, just a few steps from the well, started screaming helplessly. One of the Houdi men had grabbed her by the neck and was dragging her towards the inn. It was a shocking sight and the people around were just observing indifferently. Fortunately, at that moment, the leader of the group intervened; he went to the girl and tore her away from the hand of the Houdi man.

The Hunter watched impassively the scene and then, after the spectacle was over, he turned his gaze back to Delaida. He looked her up and down with a meaningful look and returned to the rest of his tribe. She came back to her senses and walked hurriedly to her house. The meeting with the Hunter didn't bode well. She felt that she was going to see him again, but she didn't know if she'd have the chance to escape unscathed. Once they singled someone out, the Houdi people hunted them to the end.

A few days passed, clouded by frantic concern. Delaida wanted to leave as soon as possible, so that she would not be pursued. That's why she put some clothes and a little food in a bundle and was about to leave, alone, because there was nobody to take along. But then she heard the creaking of the front step and shuddered. She saw the Hunter through a crack in the wall, he had come for her. Delaida stood on the spot and tried not to make a sound, so that he wouldn't know there was someone in the house. Cold sweat covered her forehead and hands. The Hunter knocked several times, waited for a while and then made a little step back. He began scrutinising the facade of the house. Delaida did not move. He returned to the door and sniffed like a hound. At this point, Delaida realised that he knew she was there. It was as though his sharp gaze pierced through the door, and she felt like he grabbed her. But the Hunter did nothing. He turned around and left. Today wasn't the day that he would sweep away his prey, not now. He would come back for her and she couldn't do anything. If she remained in Merab, she would fall into his clutches, and she wanted to escape far, far away and save herself from this black soul.

She waited a few minutes, which felt like hours, then she quietly left the house and took the path that led to the woods. She had to cross a broad field before entering the wild woods. Delaida walked fast and stopped only shortly, just to take her breath. The fear for her life and of her safety was choking her. She was also afraid of the wild beasts in the woods. Where would she sleep that night? Dusk was falling now. The darkness gradually covered the tops of the trees and then the rest of the forest. Delaida climbed a tree and sat down on one of its large branches. She coiled her body almost into a ball and wrapped her dress around her frozen legs. She could hear a lot of different noises, the mysterious songs of the night birds, the howling of a wolf somewhere in the distance.

She had dozed off for a while when suddenly a splash of wings over her head startled her. The night was long and cold, and the darkness impenetrable. But the morning came, and with the first rays of sunlight, Delaida set off again. She had no appetite, so she didn't stop for lunch. She walked alone for several days, and the nights she spent curled up on a tree, shivering with cold. One day her dress got caught up on a bush and when she bent down to free it, she heard human footsteps and cringed behind the bush.

She waited for a minute because she wasn't sure if she had really heard the sound. Delaida held her breath and felt her pulse thumping. But then she heard the footsteps again, and she was sure there was someone there. She couldn't peek around the bush, so she just stood up and dashed forward. Delaida was running too fast, and although she was watching her steps, she stumbled upon something and fell.

She was on her feet in a second, but then she felt two strong hands grabbing her by the shoulders and throwing her on the ground. Delaida was terrified when she saw the Hunter. He noticed the blood on her leg, leaned over and smelled it. He saw the wound from the fall, which was not deep. The Hunter stood above her and watched her without saying a word, just like a predator playing with the prey before killing her. He bent down and squeezed Delaida's wrist, staring at her with his chilling gaze. His hands were ice cold. But he did not want to kill her, he wanted to make her his own.

"I'll go gather some wood and fetch us food," he said in a commanding tone, and Delaida knew she had to obey. If she did not accept his dinner and escaped instead, she would doom herself, it meant a certain death. Houdis punished disobedience and the Houdi man would hunt her, find her and avenge the rejection.

A lot of time passed, but the Hunter hadn't yet come back. She sat curled up again, completely numb. Her mind had gone blank after the sudden encounter with the Hunter. But when evening fell and the sunset lit the sky in purple, she came a little to her senses and began to consider her options. What would happen if she stayed with the Hunter? Houdis were savage warriors, and sooner or later, he would be her undoing. And if she ran off now, the Hunter would probably catch up with her very soon and kill her on the spot that same night. In both cases, she would lose her life. Then suddenly she decided to do it anyway, to escape again. To be killed now would be a better fate than to be abused over and over again. She sprang to her feet and started running.

It got dark. It was the hardest night in Delaida's life. She didn't know how many minutes, how many seconds more she had left. Her body, frozen with fear before, was now burning. She stopped running, but continued walking. Again, the same sounds, a wolf's howl, the splash of birds' wings. It was a moonlit night. Then another sound… and she recognised it from before, it was the footsteps. She took to her heels, and then she heard the drawing and releasing of the bowstring. In a minute, she found herself lying numb on the ground and the poisoned arrow lay beside her body. The Hunter stood above Delaida, looked at her without showing any emotion and then headed back to Merab.

The whole night Delaida spent lying down in that helpless position, but she was not dead. She felt she had to fight the poison, to stay alive. Another breath of air, two more seconds of light, it was worth it to breathe, even though she was in pain. That way, on the brink of death, she drifted through the night and greeted the dawn. The sunrays fell on her, and she managed, somehow with great effort, to stand up and stumble away, to move forward. Numbness clouded everything. She didn't feel the sun nor the dark and cold, she only felt the poison that spread through her body, gnawing at her life. She walked and walked until she couldn't feel her feet anymore, and then her knees buckled and she slumped to the ground. She had no strength to stand up. She laid down, feeling the poison sucking out her forces and finally fell into the depths of unconsciousness.

And then, something pulled her out. As if in a dream, she felt the touch of warm hands to her agonising body. Someone lifted her from the cold ground and carried her...where to, she didn't know.

A young man, living in the nearby mountains, had found her in the woods and brought her home. He lived alone and nobody knew about the existence of his little hut.

When Delaida started to wake up, it was night. She opened her eyes and saw a flickering light, but she did not have the strength to keep her eyelids up. She fell back into deep slumber. Were these the last moments of her life? She had no strength to follow this thought.

And then she felt heat spreading through her body. It started from the heart and reached every last part of her. She was woken up by a soft touch to her arm. The young man stood in front of her, staring at her, slightly startled. She sat up in the bed, not knowing what to ask, and the man in front of her didn't say anything. She looked around the room she was in, and considering it didn't look dangerous, but somewhat strangely cosy with the smell of herbs and other pleasant aromas, she calmed down and asked him:

"How did I get here?"

I found you in the woods," explained the man. "You were injured and I brought you here to heal your wound. There was poison in it."

He looked at her tenderly and asked her:

"What happened to you?"

Delaida felt comfortable around this man, as if she had already known him from before. He had a pleasant-looking face and warm eyes, which made her feel safe.

"Please don't ask me about it," said Delaida, "it's a miracle you have found me and cured my poisoned body. I don't know how I can repay you for saving my life." A tear dropped from her eyes.

They kept talking for a long time and trust was born between them. He told her that his name was Evkar, he lived completely alone, and he learned from his father which herbs to pick, and how to use them in his everyday life as well as to cure various illnesses and treat wounds with them. Sometimes an elderly woman from a remote town would come for herbs to treat the people who lived in the area. She kept to herself the location of Evkar's house for his safety, so that the tribes that ruled the neighbouring lands would not force him to join them.

He offered Delaida to make her tea so that she would feel better and she accepted it with gratitude. He put it on the wooden table beside her bed and went out somewhere. Delaida drank the aromatic tea and waited for him to come back, but Evkar was late. She didn't want to stay in bed, so she got up and tried taking a few steps. She still wore her torn and bloody dress. She thought to herself that the young man had not taken it off because he didn't want to reveal her nude body. That made her smile. *Maybe he's not like other men?* she thought, and put on her shoes that he had left by the door, then went out. What a beautiful summer day it was! She breathed in deeply the fragrant warm air and felt truly alive. And somewhere near was her saviour.

She walked around the small house, which had just one room. Outside there was a little shed for the firewood. There she saw some straw on the ground and a blanket. She thought Evkar must have slept there so that she wouldn't feel threatened and worried. She decided to go to the woods to look for him, but after a while, she saw the cottage was getting too far away and got frightened. She started walking back and when she got to the house, Evkar was already there, waiting for her worriedly.

"I did not know where you were. I thought somebody found you," he said, and Delaida looked guiltily at him.

"I was quite close," she said, "I needed a little fresh air."

"Don't go alone in this forest. There are wild animals there and sometimes even scarier creatures…" said he gently, but looking very concerned.

"What do you mean?" she asked.

"Tribal warriors, armed to teeth, bloodthirsty. You'd better stay close to me, so I could help you if anything happens."

It became clear to Delaida that Evkar knew quite well about the enemy's existence, so she decided not to put either of them in danger by getting far away from the hut.

Evkar suggested that the next day he could take her to a nearby lake, where the water was crystal clear.

"We'll go to the lake; it's not far from here. It is safe there and you can bathe in it and wash your dress from the blood. I'll be waiting nearby," he offered.

Delaida gladly accepted.

It was like a new life began for Delaida in this small hut in the midst of the wild forest. The presence of this young man, who was accustomed to living alone but treated her so well, made her feel secure.

"You were unconscious for many days," said Evkar, "I wonder how you managed to recover when you're so weak. You'll need a few weeks to get healthy again." Evkar said these words in a caring tone and smiled kindly.

Delaida was moved. It felt nice to be in the company of this man and she wanted to know more of his story.

"Will you tell me about your father?" she asked.

Evkar, who was adding wood to the fireplace at that moment, stopped working and stared somewhere in the distance with a thoughtful expression on his face.

"I haven't seen him for many years," he began, and sat on the chair, "he took care for me and my mother. It were just the three of us here in this hut that he built for us. He had escaped from a tribe that took over our city. But my mother was spotted by a warrior." Evkar halted for a moment, and Delaida felt a growing tension in herself.

"This warrior wanted my mother, but when she sensed that he would try to kidnap her, she managed to get away and go to my father who, having learned about it, grabbed her and me, and without any baggage led us to the woods. He took only a few woodworking tools and a small axe. I don't remember much of the escape, because I was very little."

"What happened next?" Delaida asked anxiously.

"My father got here, and in a few days, he built the little hut," Evkar went on. Delaida stared at him with complete concentration. "The three of us lived here until I grew up. There was only one person who knew where we were – the old woman. She came to visit and brought us clothes and news from the city, and in return, we supplied her with herbs. One night, I heard the sound of horseshoes, but my father motioned me to stay inside. He went out, and I watched through a crack in the wall as my mother was thrown on the back of the horse and then the rider took her away, and my father was running after them as fast as he could. I was 13 years old at the time," Evkar was clearly reliving the experience again, as he was telling Delaida what had happened.

"I never saw my father nor my mother after that night. For days, I walked through the woods and searched for traces of them, but found nothing. I had learned from my father how to use herbs and roots that grow in the woods, which plants and fruits are not poisonous, and which are good to eat and treat illnesses and wounds. That is the way I have lived alone all these years. The only person who comes here to see me two or three times a year is the old woman."

Evkar told the story as it was paining him, and Delaida went to him and stroked his face.

"I'm sorry your life was so bitter, Evkar," she said, looking gently at him.

After dinner, Delaida lay calmly on the bed of straw, and Evkar went outside. The night was pleasant and brought a fresh morning. She was awakened by the scent of food. They had breakfast and, after that, headed to the lake. When they arrived there, Evkar gave her privacy and sat not far away while she was bathing. Delaida felt protected, knowing he was nearby.

After she went out of the water, Evkar moved a little closer to her. Delaida felt she wanted to embrace him, but refrained to do so. Evkar also looked stirred by the same emotion.

The days went by, Evkar was taking good care of her. Affection was born and started to grow between them. They began to go out to the forest for herbs, prepare meals together, and laugh together. The barriers fell and both of them wanted to move forward to the next stage after friendship. He was a strong young man, and she was an attractive woman. But they still held back.

One night, Delaida stayed alone in the room, while Evkar went to get water from the well, which was not far away. It took him quite long, and she began to worry about him. Finally, he appeared, left the bucket of water, closed the door, and spoke:

"Delaida, I don't know how it happened that our paths crossed," he began, "I lived alone for ten years, and I thought I was going to be alone for the rest of my life. But you appeared in my life and it changed completely. Now I want to be with you, I want you to never leave. Please stay with me..."

It was such an intense moment, a turning point in both of their lives. Delaida listened with excitement. She came to him, gently caressed his face and hugged him. This embrace was full of passion and comfort. Now she could hear Evkar's breathing, she felt the warmth of his hands on her shoulders; then, he slowly moved his palms down her body and rested them on her hips. She was perfectly happy with his touch and stood on her toes for the first kiss they shared.

The Hunter returned to the forest with a group of men from his tribe. They hunted for food, but they also killed animals just for the fun of it.

It was early morning when the Hunter saw the old woman who had been to Evkar's hut for herbs and was now walking slowly down the mountain path towards the town. He and his hunting party surrounded her. All these fierce warriors on their strong horses looked sinister and the woman was terrified.

"Where do you come from, old hag," commanded the Hunter, eyeing her with his fierce glance.

"I was picking herbs in the woods," answered the old woman, pale with fear.

"You've gotten quite far for such an old woman," the Hunter said, "is there anyone else with you?"

"I came here alone, away in the mountains, to pick herbs near the lake," she repeated, not knowing she was giving away the place where Evkar lived.

"I didn't know there was a lake in this mountain," said the Hunter.

"It is just a small lake," she said in a shaking voice.

And then the old woman tried to leave, but two horsemen stood in her way.

"Let her go," said the Hunter, and motioned to his people to follow him.

His instinct of a pursuer told him there was something about the lake the old woman was trying to hide. He and the other horsemen broke into a gallop towards it. They reached the lake when it was already dark. The Hunter ordered them to make a fire and roast the game, and he went on his own to explore the vicinity. The sounds of wild animals and the howling of wolves increased the thrill of pursuing something unknown.

Evkar and Delaida were in the hut and did not suspect that danger was approaching. It was already completely dark when the Hunter saw a faint crack of light in the distance. He found the hut and within a few minutes, he stood in front of it. He heard the voices of a man and a woman inside. Suddenly, the Hunter heard a growl near him and barely managed to turn around when a wolf leaped at him and buried its teeth in his hand. He managed to get his knife out and cut the wolf's throat, and the animal fell down, whining helplessly. Evkar heard an unusual sound and knew something was not right, so he motioned to Delaida to stay in the hut, and he went out with a torch in his hand. He found the dead animal in front of the house, but there was no one around.

Evkar knew that the hut was found by one of the Houdi people, who had killed the wolf and had left for now. But he would, without a doubt, come back.

That night would be the last Evkar was going to spend in the hut. Early in the morning, he and Delaida would head east through the mountains, to seek a new shelter.

The Hunter returned to his men. Blood ran down his hand, and he wrapped his wound with some cloth. He would come back to the hut the next day and this time he would not just stand outside.

When Delaida saw the dead wolf, she somehow felt the Hunter was nearby. Neither she nor Evkar was able to sleep that night, but they lay close to each other, tangled in a tight embrace. Whatever happened to them, they were already together, and they were ready to meet even death. Before the sun rose, they gathered what they would need for the journey and started on their way through the mountains.

The Hunter sent his men to the city, and although the wound on his hand was deep, he climbed onto his horse and went to the hut. He broke the door and saw that there was no one inside. He examined the objects left inside and smelled the straw on the bed. This smell was familiar. He had not found Delaida's dead body in the woods when he returned before, and now he was sure she was alive.

He started pursuing her again.

Some years ago, Evkar had built a hidden shelter in a few hours' walk from the hut. He had dug a tunnel leading to an underground cave that was large enough to accommodate two people. He had brought in everything needed for surviving. There were blankets on the ground to sleep on, and even a small table and wooden utensils. On the other side, there was a second tunnel that could be used in case of danger. Since they weren't far ahead from the Hunter, Evkar decided they should stay in the underground hiding place until the enemy passed them by.

Delaida was shaking, chills running down her body. She felt like a deer chased by a pack of wolves, but having Evkar beside her gave her strength to move forward. Now their once separate lives had become one.

"You are no longer alone, Delaida, I will do everything in my power to protect you." Evkar hugged her hard and kissed her forehead. "Before I met you, I didn't know how lonely I was. Now you are my life and even if I have just one day left, I'll be happy to live it with you."

So, they promised to stay together, whatever may happen to them.

They stayed in the underground hiding place for two days. Then they ran out of food and had to continue their journey. Evkar wanted to go out early at sunrise, and hunt some small animal down by himself, but Delaida didn't want to leave him alone. Evkar went out first and reached for Delaida's hand. She felt as if her heart was going to burst, as if an arrow would suddenly spring out of somewhere and pierce Evkar's or her own body. They looked around, but there was no one outside. Then they headed up the mountains where the great river flowed.

There, Evkar caught some fish and started a fire to roast it. The two sat down for a very short time, just to have a quick breakfast. He put two fish in his bag, so they wouldn't have to stop for hunting or fishing later. Then they had to cross the river, but they did not have a boat. The place was quite desolate and there was no one nearby. During his many years of solitude, Evkar had come here many times and had built a small raft which he had buried purposely, and now it proved quite useful. He and Delaida get onto the raft and started sailing, but when they were in the middle of the river, they saw the Hunter standing at the spot they had set off from.

He stood on the shore and stared at them. Delaida saw him first and squeezed Evkar's hand hard. Tears sprang to her eyes and she looked at him helplessly. He glared at the Hunter who had already lifted the bow and directed it toward them, and he told Delaida to swiftly jump into the river and catch the board of the raft. The two of them jumped, and at that moment, two arrows flew over their heads. They had to swim the rest of the distance to the other side, clutching the rim of the raft and looking back to the Hunter. The water was ice cold, and when they arrived on the opposite bank, Delaida passed out on the ground.

Evkar cupped her face in his hands and tried to wake her up, calling her name. Then he carried her up the slope, stripped off her wet clothes, covered her with autumn leaves to warm her up and set a fire next to her. He took off his own clothes and left them by the fire to dry. Then he lay beside her, embracing her to warm up her body with his. A few hours later, she woke up and asked him what had happened after they arrived on the opposite bank. He explained that she had lost consciousness and that despite the ordeal they were now safe.

"The Hunter will not be able to follow us until he makes a raft himself, and he will need at least one day for that. We'll head east where there's a small town at the foot of the mountains. We will stay there for a few days," Evkar said, stroking her face.

They spent the night at this place, and the next day they set off again. They were walking fast, and though their bodies were tired, their willpower made them continue their escape without allowing longer breaks. In the evening, they lay side by side and kept themselves warm by clinging their bodies together.

Four days later, they saw the city in the distance. They were only a few hours away.

The two stood, facing each other, held their hands and looked into each other's eyes.

"Evkar, I would not have survived without you," Delaida said, her eyes filling with tears.

"I feel as if I've been preparing for our escape my entire lifetime," Evkar said, and leaned in to kiss her. It was then when he heard the footsteps and instinctively stood before Delaida. This move saved her from being shot in the heart, but Evkar was hit on the shoulder. Delaida fell silent, but seeing the man, who was now dearer to her than her own life, with a poisoned arrow in his flesh, a blazing fire violently roared through her, and she felt a surge of power.

Even though Evkar was a tall and strong man, the poison of the arrow that dug deeply in his shoulder would spread soon and weaken him. Delaida shrieked and ran to the nearby tree that the Hunter had used as a cover. She was running in zigzag so she would confuse him and he could not aim directly at her. Evkar swayed, but was still conscious; he trod after her. She reached the Hunter, who did not expect his 'prey' to attack him, and managed to grab him by the neck. She clutched with all her strength. The Hunter was much stronger than she was, and if Evkar was not near, he would break her in a few moments, but Evkar had found a heavy piece of wood and now swung it in his hand, and when the Hunter caught her by the neck and knocked her down, Evkar hit him on head, hard.

The Hunter turned his head and looked at him with a furious look. Evkar hit him once more, and blood flowed from the Hunter's ear. Evkar swayed, the poison already clouding his mind and vision, carrying him away. He dropped the piece of wood and began to fight with the Hunter, whose hand was still wounded by the wolf bite. The two men fought fiercely. Delaida had come to her senses and went behind Evkar, then pulled the arrow out of his shoulder. He screamed from the severe pain, and gripped the Hunter even harder. But this effort depleted his forces completely, and the Hunter knocked him down on the ground. Delaida threw herself at the Hunter and thrust the arrow, which had stabbed Evkar, into the Hunter's neck. He turned to her and looked at her with the savage gaze of a dying predator. He pulled the arrow out of his neck, but it opened a deep wound and the Hunter lost too much blood. He was defeated, and Delaida watched her assassin die from the arrow he had aimed at her.

Evkar barely moved and Delaida got really scared. She approached him and said,

"Tell me what is the healing herb for this poison and where to find it!" she screamed desperately.

"Whether I stay alive or die, I want you to know that I love you," said Evkar, who was almost unconscious.

"Tell me what the herb is," Delaida shouted, shaking Evkar. He whispered in Delaida's ear the name of the herb, and fell unconscious.

Delaida saw Evkar's eyes close. She felt a new surge of power and began to look for the herb that Evkar told her to use. She knew what it looked like, and that it could be found near rivers or lakes, so she furiously began to run, looking for the plant.

Delaida wandered and searched for a nearby stream or lake. She had come so far away into the woods that she did not know if she could find the way back, and that frightened her.

She fell to the ground and had the feeling that her heart would jump out of her chest when she saw a young deer going east. She stood quietly and began to follow it. Not long after, the deer had led her to a clear stream, and Delaida rushed along its brink to seek the herb. Near the small waterfall, there was a large tree wrapped in ivy. She went to it and there, at its roots, she found the healing plant. She picked some of it and then drank from the water thirstily before she rushed back down the forest, sweating all over.

It was almost dark, and she could see the sunset going down under the horizon. The journey back seemed endless, and there somewhere lay the man she loved, the man who had saved her life. Delaida didn't stop for a break, and as the time passed it was getting colder. She started shivering, chills ran down her body. All the trees in the woods looked the same, and she was confused where to go. She wished that it was just a bad dream and she would wake up sooner. She had no other choice but to follow her heart and it led her to Evkar.

It was already dark when she got back and threw her arms around him. She felt his body was getting colder and began to squeeze the herb through tears. She gently put a few of its leaves over the wound and then started a fire. She pressed a piece of burning wood to the wound to mix the herb with the fresh blood. Now all she could do was to wait. She lay down by the fire beside Evkar, closing her tired eyes.

The sun was on the horizon when Delaida felt a warm hand embracing her. She turned and saw Evkar's pleasant face, slightly smiling. She smiled back.

The Frozen Prince

There once was a kingdom far away at the end of the world where eternal winter reigned. Snow covered the earth and the streets were made out of ice. Trees covered in hoar frost and thousands of snowflakes resembled works of art, which nature had formed according to its own taste.

In this kingdom, even the people had hearts of ice. Nobody could feel deep or warm feelings, and love was something like a legend of times long gone.

In a tiny little house on the edge of town lived a small family, man and wife together with their daughter Deria, who was the only wealth they had.

On a particularly frosty day, when a furious and pitiless wind was blowing, Deria had been caught out in the snowstorm, and was seeking a place where she could hide. Threatened by strong winds, Deria felt frost start to cover her face and eyes. She sought shelter at an icy door, which had attracted her attention. The door opened to a tunnel where she had never been before. Deria leaned on the door, opened it slightly and looked around, but she couldn't see anything in the darkness. She wondered where the tunnel might lead. A few snowflakes coming from inside the tunnel fell on her face.

The pathway must lead somewhere, she thought and decided to solve the riddle. So, she made a few steps and soon saw light before her. As she got further through the tunnel, she noticed that there were increasingly more snowflakes blowing past. After a few moments, Deria saw that she had reached a frozen garden. She had not known anything about the existence of this place. As a child, with her friends she was discovering and exploring many secret places, and she knew all hidden things of the kingdom, but never had she gotten into this garden. Neither had anybody talked to her about it.

A beautiful tree was situated in the middle. The branches stretched out in an elegant way and there were little blossoms all over it. The tree admonished of past times, a forgotten spring. While Deria looked at the blossoms with interest and curiously absorbed every detail of the beautiful tree, her eyes stopped at something, which was to be seen behind it. There was a statue made out of ice. Deria went nearer and began to examine it. It was the statue of a young man, a beautiful piece of art. She couldn't stop looking at the masterfully made statue which seemed so real. Deria reached out her hand to touch the face of the young man and caressed his icy skin.

That day she stayed in the hidden garden for hours. She came to her senses when it was nearly dark outside and her hands were freezing cold. Leaving the place, she saw that the blossoms on the tree had closed up.

When she came home, her parents were angry. As people with frozen hearts, they did not have understanding for each other or for her. Deria was sad about that and felt in her heart that the way this world worked wasn't right.

She went into her little room and snuggled up under the blanket.

The encounter with the frozen statue took hold of her thoughts entirely. She wanted to fall asleep quicker, so that tomorrow will come sooner and she could return to the mysterious garden. She closed her eyes and pictured the statue of the young man. Thoughts about him carried her into sweet sleep.

Streets were covered in ice and children were sliding on them. People were wearing ice skates instead of shoes. Deria hurried to reach the tunnel and spent the day in the hidden garden, next to the statue. The garden had become her hiding place, where she could be in peace, far away from the cold-hearted people and where time seemed to have stopped. She could share her thoughts with the frozen prince as she called him, although he couldn't talk back.

One day, she stayed there longer than usual and darkness covered the land, so Deria couldn't see the tunnel to get home. But how could she stay outside in the night when no human being could survive the cold? She sat close to the young frozen man, huddled up.

"Oh, handsome prince, you don't feel the cold, do you?" she said smiling at the statue, as if it could hear her.

"Be careful not to make the prince feel too proud of himself," said a very soft voice from somewhere near. Deria looked around but didn't see anybody.

"I am here, close to you!" A little white bird had landed on the shoulder of the frozen statue. "Apparently the two of us will keep each other company tonight," it continued. Daria was surprised to see this peculiar talking bird and was wondering where did it come from.

"I've been seeing you coming here," began the little white bird and shook its wings. Its feathers were golden and this amazed the girl even more. "I am sure you want to know the story of the frozen prince," said the bird and came closer to her. "Yes, I would very much want to know his story," said Deria and looked at the prince with eyes full of affection.

"It all began with a king and a queen, who loved each other very much, and dreamed of having a child. Many years they were hoping to be blessed with a beautiful prince who will make their life full and complete, but as the years went by, they lost hope. The queen dreamed to see what her grown up son would look like and the king ordered the best craftsman in the kingdom to make a statue, which would resemble him and his queen. The craftsman was honoured to be given such an important task. He worked day and night to complete it with the greatest craftsmanship he could.

When the statue was ready, he went to the palace and placed it before the king and his queen. He took away the veil to reveal the face of the young man made out of ice. Cold wind burst into the great hall and fluttered the young man's cloak. The queen was stunned, seeing the handsome face of the young man. She felt love in her heart, seeing the beautiful statue of her son. How she longed for him to be alive.

Not long after, spring came and the weather gradually became warmer. The king and the queen were worried what will happen to the prince. The last thing they wanted was he to melt, so they decided to take him to a cold land. They became aware of the Ice kingdom and ordered a secret garden to be built far away from people's eyes where their ice son will be hidden, away and safe. In the garden, they planted a small tree as a memory from his loving parents.

The king and his queen returned to their kingdom and didn't go back to the secret garden.

As years passed, the tree grew and became the only companion of the frozen prince."

"This is the story of the statue Deria!" said the bird.

"How come you know my name?" she asked, astonished.

"I know a lot of things about this cold world, how hard it is to discover a warm place here. But in your heart there is so much warmth, enough to melt even a frozen heart!"

Deria did not know what to say. The story the little bird told her was so wonderful and left her speechless. Deep inside, she felt the frozen prince wasn't just a piece of ice and that thought carried her to a dream which she didn't want to end.

Morning came and Deria rubbed her eyes sleepily. She had fallen asleep at some point and felt good and peaceful. She caressed the face of the prince tenderly and headed to the house of her parents. She didn't feel home there, as she felt she belonged to the secret garden and her prince.

A group of children saw her leaving the garden, and without hesitation, they stormed into the tunnel, discovering the tree and the frozen prince. They screamed and called even more people to come to the place. A crowd of people gathered and they wondered what this frozen figure might be.

"Perhaps it has been thrown out by a sculptor who didn't like it anymore," said someone. "Or it is the unsuccessful product of art students who waste their time doing useless things like that," thought others. But nobody could appreciate the distinguished look of the frozen prince. People saw it only as a piece of ice, worked out by human hands.

Deria didn´t stay home long before she returned to her prince. From a distance, she saw a crowd of people at the tunnel, and was afraid what they could have done? She rushed into the garden, making way through the crowd and saw a few children pulling on the hand of the statue. She was scared they might damage it and ran to protect it. She stood in front of the frozen prince, exposed to the public gaze.

"What do you think you are doing, girl?" asked someone with an impudent tone.

"This is my prince, and I am not going to allow anybody to damage him!" she said in a determined tone.

"Why don't you move this useless work or should I say waste of art out of here?" said a man with a vile facial expression. There began a hustle and bustle among the people, and they knocked the statue to the ground. Somebody threw a stone at the prince and a chip of ice cracked off the prince's chest.

Deria was petrified and threw herself onto the frozen price to stop them from destroying him completely.

Her sad look and her pathetic devotion to this frozen statue made the crowd lose interest and gradually they began to leave the garden, until only

Deria alone remained. A cold winter night covered the earth with a black curtain. Deria lost sense of time. She felt every beat of her heart and felt she could not continue to live if the icy prince would be destroyed. He was her special companion who brought warmth in her life. Deria felt helpless and weak. She couldn't even raise the icy figure to put it back to its place. A tear, hot like fire, rolled down her face and dropped into the little hole in the prince's chest and went straight into his heart.

The tear turned into a blue flame, and all of a sudden, the whole statue changed in colour. Deria saw how warm ivory skin was covering the face of the frozen prince and then his arms and legs, until the frozen statue became a real human being. She looked into the face of the young man, her tears stopped out of surprise.

Deria couldn't believe her eyes. There he stood, a wonderful young man, her precious prince. She couldn't comprehend how that was possible, when she recalled the words of the little bird with golden wings who said, "In your heart there is so much warmth to melt even a frozen heart."

"I greet you," said the prince in a velvety voice, "how I longed for this moment to come," and he embraced the girl tenderly, keeping her close to him. In this moment, the ice tree began to come to life, the ice flowers turned into beautiful blossoms and the whole garden transferred into beautiful spring.

"I thank you for melting my frozen heart with your love. Allow me to give you my love in return, I want to share my life with you and to grow old together," said the prince and took Deria's hand.

In the Ice kingdom happened a real wonder. One human heart filled with love gave the gift of life to a frozen heart. The handsome prince brought Deria home to his parents, the king and his queen. Seeing her son come back to her alive made the queen feel overwhelmed with joy, and she cried and laughed at the same time.

The king and the queen accepted Deria with great joy and loved her very much.

She was no longer just a girl with a warm heart in the fiercely cold world, she was greatly cherished and loved and gave love in return with all her heart and soul. The prince and Deria lived a life full of joy and happiness and brought hope and warmth to everyone who heard their story.

The Elixir

In a faraway kingdom, a story was told about The Black Prince who had the most enchanting eyes and who all girls dreamed of marrying. But once they looked into his eyes closely, fear enveloped their hearts.

The Black Prince was very powerful, and he could choose for his wife any maiden he wanted from the kingdom.

But so it happened that one day while the prince was hunting for deer, he was badly injured by the horns of a large stag. His servants could not help him, and they were afraid that the prince wouldn't live for long after being so badly wounded.

Not far from the forest where the hunt was, there was a small village where the servants brought the wounded prince to seek help. A young maiden saw the royal retinue carrying him and called her brothers for help. They took the Black Prince to their little house, and the girl who had brought up her younger brothers as her own children started taking care of the Prince's wounds. While she was bandaging his wounds she noticed that the blood dripping from them was black in colour. The girl was very surprised to see that, but gently took care of the injured prince.

The royal servant waited outside, and when the girl came out, he asked her:

"Is the prince still alive," he said with an anxious voice.

"He is badly injured I'm afraid, but in a few days we will know if he'll survive," she said.

In the evening, she watched over the Black Prince and prepared a special herbal infusion so he would regain his strength. But since he lay motionless, the girl dripped a few drops of potion on his lips.

A few days passed during which the girl was taking care of the Black Prince's wounds. One day, as she sprinkled again a few drops from the potion on his lips, the prince suddenly opened his eyes and caught her wrist. The girl got startled and froze. When she looked into his eyes, they were like a mirror to some unknown world. The Prince spoke:

"Who are you?" He said, and started to stand up, but sharp ache cut him off, and he let go of the girl's wrist and frowned in pain.

"My name is Anastasia, and I've been looking after you for the last few days since they brought you wounded by a deer," she said, and sat down in the chair beside him, "I put herbal potion on your lips that helps you recover."

The prince closed his eyes with pain, and soon fell into a restless sleep. Anastasia prepared soup for the prince and served it to him when he woke up.

The next day, one of the girl's younger brothers looked curiously through the door at the prince, but got scared when he returned his gaze and ran away. The prince turned to Anastasia:

"Who are you and what is your story?" He asked.

"You already know my name. I have been living here since my parents abandoned me in the woods. I've been found when I was two or three years old, and I have no memories from my birth parents. I was raised by the people who found me and grew up with their seven sons who were like real brothers to me. Unfortunately, we were orphaned six years ago, and I had to take care of the younger ones. The boy who peeked through the door was the youngest, Jonas."

The Prince listened to her carefully, but showed no emotion. And every time she looked into his eyes, Anastasia seemed to get lost in this unfamiliar world that was peering through them.

The Black Prince stayed for a few days in the small house, but once he felt better, his servants prepared a carriage to take him to the palace. Anastasia's seven brothers were standing in a row, the smallest Jonas did not dare to look into the eyes of this mysterious prince. They all bowed to him and wished him quick recovery.

Anastasia held in her hands a small bottle in which she had prepared the herbal potion. Now she handed it to the prince:

"This will help you get better soon," she whispered.

The Black Prince did not show any emotion, but he looked into Anastasia's eyes for a long moment until she felt uneasy and her cheeks flushed.

"We'll see each other again, Anastasia," he said, and motioned to the servants to carry him away.

After the Black Prince left, Anastasia could not stop thinking about him and the words he said to her. What did he mean saying that they would see each other again? Did he plan to go hunting in the nearby woods once he got better and would he come to the village again?

She was fascinated by his eyes and felt the thrill of blooming love, a new and unfamiliar feeling for the young lass.

Few months passed and then one day, returning from the forest where she had been gathering wild fruit, Anastasia saw little Jonas running towards her very excitedly.

"What happened?" Anastasia asked with astonishment, and Jonas, barely breathing, announced that a royal messenger was waiting for her at home with confidential news.

Anastasia felt a warm wave pass through her and hurriedly went to the house.

When she arrived, the royal messenger stood up and bowed slightly. Anastasia was surprised because royal messengers did not usually bow to ordinary people. She left the basket of wild fruit on the floor and approached the messenger.

"Milady," he began with an official tone, "I have been sent to you to relay a message from the Black Prince."

Anastasia felt her heart beating fast. The royal messenger took out a scroll tied with a black ribbon, untied it and started reading:

"The throne that belongs to my future betrothed was vacant for a long time. I will welcome the moment you will take this place, beside me."

Anastasia felt weakness in her knees and thought she had to sit down because it seemed so unbelievable. She, who was abandoned in the woods when she was a little girl, to become the one the mighty prince chose? In her mind, his eyes appeared, eyes so deep that seemed to draw her to him with an invisible thread.

Anastasia accepted the Prince's invitation with excitement, mingled with fear. She was ready to go the next day. It made her sad that she had to leave her beloved brothers behind but she promised to send them invitations to visit her in the palace. The thought of being the chosen one by the Black Prince made her feel flattered, but the unfamiliar direction in which she would go from here filled her soul with unceasing excitement and anxiousness. Anastasia could not sleep well, dreaming of his hypnotic, deep eyes.

In the morning, a carriage was waiting for her, all draped in black satin. How beautiful and elegant this carriage was, and inside there was a black velvet dress left for her, embroidered with precious stones. There was also a hair accessory – a small elegant tiara. Anastasia changed into her new clothes and bid farewell to her brothers.

The trip to the palace lasted only a day and so Anastasia, the royal messenger and the coachmen arrived at sunset. She was stunned by the beauty of the castle - the last rays of sunlight lit up the tops of the towers and made the view really impressive. She felt so tiny in comparison to this huge palace and its spacious gardens with hedge mazes. Anastasia climbed the steps of the castle and the huge gates opened in front of her. She was led to a spacious hall where she had to wait for the Black Prince. The walls of the hall were beautifully painted with colourful drawings depicting scenes of folk legends, and seven hallways branched out of the hall, decorated with chandeliers of different colours. Anastasia studied the pictures with interest, and they seemed to come to life in front of her. She was fascinated by the stories they were telling.

"Remarkable," Anastasia heard the Prince's voice and turned to see if he was behind her, but he wasn't there. She heard his footsteps and looked around to see where they came from, but she didn't know which corridor he would use.

"You look remarkable, Anastasia. "Said the prince while walking toward her.

Anastasia felt chills of excitement run through her body.

"Thank you," she said in a low voice and blushed.

The prince came close to her and took her hand in his, gazing into her eyes.

"It is interesting how a moment of life can be immortalized through art," noted Anastasia, " I wonder when they were painted?"

"These paintings tell the stories of my predecessors and they were painted in the course of centuries. One day, my portrait will be among them, and I will be depicted on it with my chosen one - the prince brought Anastasia's hand to his lips and gently kissed it, then led her to the dining room.

The dinner was so exquisite, the table full of sophisticated dishes and fruits that Anastasia had never tasted. It was very pleasant to her to be close to the prince, but she could not eat much because of excitement.

She felt beautiful, wearing the dress the Black Prince had given her, and she noticed that he was looking at her with passion.

After dinner, she was taken to her chambers, where the walls were clothed in black velvet. The room was very spacious and had a large window she could see the starry sky through. Anastasia lay down on the large bed and thought of the handsome prince. She was absorbed by a sweet feeling which quickly brought sleep to her eyes.

In the morning, Anastasia was awakened by the song of birds. She got up and looked out of the window. The branches of a big tree touched the castle wall and she saw many birds that lived amongst them.

Under the door of the room, she found a letter with black seal and opened it. It read:

"Now that you are with me, there is no need to waste time on preparations. In seven days, our wedding will take place here in the palace, and you will be forever mine. This evening there will be a ball in your honour. You will find your dress for the event in the wardrobe. "

Anastasia opened the closet and saw that there were many pretty dresses in it, all in black. Some were elegant but casual, others glittering with precious stones and stunningly beautiful. She saw a note on one of them saying it was specially prepared for the evening. Its neckline was richly embroidered with sparkling emeralds that glowed beautifully.

Anastasia chose one of the elegant casual dresses and went for a walk through the palace. It was very interesting to explore everything. The corridors were spacious, the ceiling was very high, and chandeliers embellished with precious stones hung from it. There were paintings on the walls, and in the corners - tall vases of flowers. It seemed as if the castle was uninhabited, she didn't see a single servant in the corridors. She had been walking for quite some time, when she noticed that one of the corridors was completely dark. She stopped for a moment and looked in that direction. Somewhere in the distance she saw a faint blue light. She looked around and, seeing no one, entered the corridor. A sense of fear enveloped her, but also some kind of curiosity. She reached the end of the corridor and stopped in front of an open door. A fireplace was blazing with a blue flame that lit the room, which wasn't very large. In the room there was a bookcase, a writing table with an ink-pot and feathers on it, and an open book. Anastasia approached the table and peered into the book.

There she saw words written in unknown language and a drawing of a bottle. Under the drawing she read: *"Seven kisses. Ambrosiae antidotos."*

She also noticed that in the room, there was a shelf above the table on which there were seven small bottles of the same shape as the one in the book. They were filled with liquid that glowed with blue light.

Anastasia reached and took one of the bottles. Then she heard some noise and got scared. She hid behind the door and held her breath, putting the small glass bottle in her pocket. She stood there and waited for a few minutes, then she came quietly out of the corridor and headed to her room.

She walked past the dining room and smelled the delicious aroma of food. By the door stood the royal messenger who had accompanied her during her journey to the castle. Breakfast was served, and he invited her to the dining room.

"Good Morning Milady," he said politely, "breakfast is served, and you can take your place."

It was only then Anastasia realized how hungry she was, and thanked the courtier. She looked around, searching for the prince.

"The prince will not join you for breakfast," the courtier said.

It was very surprising to her that she would have breakfast alone and she felt somewhat awkward. She was accustomed to eating with her brothers, who were always very cheerful, and now she was completely alone in the big dining room. But the delicious food and the rays of sunlight coming through the window made her feel better.

When she finished her breakfast and left the dining room, Anastasia saw the halls buzzing with people. The servants who were nowhere to be seen earlier, now were in a hurry decorating the palace for the ball that night, an event that would bring here all the nobles from the neighbouring kingdoms.

Anastasia retired to her room when she saw that the bustle grew even bigger.

She took the glass container out of her pocket, examined it, and noticed that the liquid was no longer shining in blue. Then she hid the bottle in the wardrobe.

When the evening came and Anastasia put on the emerald embellished dress, she heard a knock on the door. She opened it and saw the Black Prince standing in front of her, tall, charming and glamorous. When she saw him, her breath caught, he was so handsome that she did not know how to control her excitement of his presence.

"You look astonishing Anastasia," he noted, stepping forward and kissed her cheek.

Her heart almost jumped out of her chest. She had fallen madly in love with the prince and felt greatly attracted to him. She breathed in, his aroma was as enchanting as he himself.

He took her hand and they headed for the throne room.

When they entered through the great gate, all guests stopped their conversations to look at the Black Prince's chosen one. She held his hand tightly. The two of them looked very beautiful together and all the guests were watching them with admiration. It was their first night as fiancés. The Black Prince asked Anastasia for a dance and while dancing with him, she felt as if she was getting lost in some unknown and magical world.

A young man dressed in white was standing in one of the corners of the room and was watching the couple. After the dance ended, Anastasia went to get herself a glass of wine, although she was already intoxicated by the presence of the Black Prince next to her. The man in white approached her and said:

"My greetings for the engagement, Anastasia". He took her hand, kissed it and then bowed slightly.

As if awakened from a dream, Anastasia only now noticed the young man.

"Thank you," she said, a little embarrassed, "forgive me, but I do not know you?"

"I am the Prince of the White Kingdom, Erik," he bowed once more.

"Nice to meet you, Erik."

"The pleasure is all mine," he said, smiling gently.

She did not notice when the Black Prince came near, but she felt someone grabbed her by the shoulder, and when she turned around, she saw her fiancé. The Black Prince nodded in acknowledgement of the Prince of the White Kingdom but it was just a courtesy. It was obvious that there was tension between them. The Black Prince spoke no word, but he put his arm around Anastasia's waist, and didn't let go for the rest of the evening.

When the ball was over, the Black Prince accompanied Anastasia to her room. He leaned towards her and looked into her eyes, then he put his hands on her shoulders, and smoothly slid them down to her hips. Anastasia shivered, feeling as if burning with excitement. Then he pressed her against his body and touched her lips with his. This first kiss was so passionate that Anastasia felt like she was entirely his and wanted to give herself to him completely. When he wished her a good night and walked down the corridor, Anastasia went dizzily into her room and sank straight into bed as she felt a little lightheaded.

It was during this night when she felt a piercing pain that shot through her heart and woke her up. She barely managed to take a breath, when another sharp pain pierced her body. She did not know what was going on with her, but she felt like she was dying. The pain grew stronger, and she couldn't even gather the strength to move. Then she saw something in the wardrobe flashing blue. While looking toward the blue light, she felt the pain cease for a moment, and then it cut her again. She got up trembling and staggered to the wardrobe, but there she slipped to the floor in pain. She saw that the blue light was coming from the liquid in the bottle she had stacked away in the closet. She had little power left in her and with one last effort she grabbed the glass bottle and drank the liquid. Immediately she felt that the piercing pain started to disappear. Exhausted, she lost consciousness.

As the rays of the sun penetrated the curtains and lit up Anastasia's exhausted body, she opened her eyes and rose from the ground, still holding the empty glass bottle in her hand. She felt dizzy and could not comprehend what had happened to her. Everything she remembered from last evening was the Black Prince's intoxicating eyes and his fiery kiss. Then she recalled the piercing pain and that the blue liquid she drank saved her life.

She opened the curtains and looked through the window, it was a beautiful day. Then she saw a white horse in the garden which was looking at her. After a few moments of just staring, the horse bowed slightly which surprised her and made her smile.

Anastasia got dressed and left the room. She did not know what had caused the sharp pain in her heart, but she knew she had to get more of this elixir because the luminous blue liquid had saved her, although she had no idea how it worked. She remembered what was written in the book: "*Seven kisses, Anbrosiae antidodos*". Anastasia walked quietly down the dark corridor, but this time she did not see the blue light from afar because the door was closed. Slowly moving and full of fear, she reached the end of the corridor and saw a slightly flickering light through a small crack below the door. She pushed the door and it opened. Anastasia came in and saw that the book was not on the table, but the six small bottles were still where she had seen them yesterday. She picked up all of them and put them in her dress pocket, but before she left, she searched feverishly the library for a book that could explain the meaning of "*Ambrosiae antidotos*". Despite her efforts, she couldn't find any book in understandable language, but she still picked up an ancient looking book with a very strange, worn-out cover... And then, suddenly, the Black Prince walked through the door. Anastasia froze with the book in her hands, and he just stared at her with an odd look in his eyes.

"Are you looking for something, Anastasia?" asked the prince, without taking his eyes off her.

Anastasia felt cold sweat dripping down her forehead. But she thought the elixir bottles were safe in her pocket and hoped that the book would conceal their blue light.

"I was walking around the palace... and I came to this corridor. I saw there was a library here and..." Anastasia stopped at this because she did not want to reveal she had discovered the blue potion.

The Black Prince came to her and took the book from her hands. Anastasia held her breath, afraid that he would see the blue light, but he turned around and put the book back on the shelf. While he had his back on her, she rearranged the pleats of her dress to hide the faint blue light.

"I'll show you the library of the palace, which has many more books. You should not come here anymore," the Black Prince said firmly, his voice menacing. Then he added he would join Anastasia for dinner.

She understood that he was dismissing her and quietly left the room.

Anastasia hurried to her bedroom and hid the elixir bottles. When she had stacked them safely into the closet, she sat down on the bed and took a deep breath. She was not sure what was going on, she was afraid deep down, but at the same time she felt an incredibly strong attraction to the Black

Prince, and she waited to become his wife with great excitement.

A slight knock drew her attention to the window. She went to it and saw that a little white bird had perched on the ledge and was looking at her. She opened the window, and the bird bowed slightly, then flew away. A large white feather was left on the ledge of the window, and on it, in gold letters, was written:

"Tomorrow at sunset, meet me in the garden below your bedroom."

Anastasia wondered who had sent this feather with a message for her, and why did they invite her to meet them in the garden?

The evening came and she put on an elegant silk black dress and went to dinner.

The Black Prince looked as fascinating as ever, and he greeted her at the door, giving her a beautiful rose. The food was delicious, and Anastasia was so enthralled by the pleasant atmosphere that she completely forgot all her fears. After dinner, the Black Prince invited her to the throne room.

"I want to show you something, Anastasia. Do me the honour to come with me, "he said gallantly, and offered her his hand.

The two then went to the throne room, where the Black Prince gave her a sign to wait for him. The light was dimmed, and the shadows of the big columns gathered in the middle of the great hall, shaping strange silhouettes. The Black Prince came back in a moment and opened a large velvet box in front of her, which contained the most beautiful necklace Anastasia had ever seen – a string of black sapphires that sparked amazingly even in this faint light.

"This necklace is a present for our wedding which will be in 5 nights," the Black Prince declared.

"Thank you, it is incredible... I am... very flattered...," she pronounced shyly.

"You will be the most beautiful bride," he whispered in her ear, and then kissed her passionately on the lips.

A little later, Anastasia returned to her bedroom, accompanied by a royal maid who was carrying the box with the wedding necklace. The maid left the box on the dressing table and closed the door behind her as she left the room. Anastasia lay on the bed, feeling sweet intoxication enveloping her again. She fell into a deep sleep and dreamed of dancing with the Black Prince when suddenly the same piercing pains cut through her heart and woke her up. She knew right away that she had only a few seconds to get to the elixir in the closet, or her life would have ended at this very moment. She managed to grab one of the bottles that were glowing in bright blue now, and drank it with her last ounce of strength.

In the morning, Anastasia was woken up by the gentle sun rays caressing her body. She rose from the ground, then looked at the empty bottle. She could not fathom what was going on, what was happening to her. She looked into the wardrobe and saw that there were 5 elixir bottles left there, exactly as the number of days left till the wedding with the Black Prince.

The day passed quickly. The Black Prince had ordered Anastasia to be taken to the great library while she didn't know where the Prince himself was. Anastasia liked the library very much and stayed there the whole day until sunset. Then she left the room and went to the palace gates. She wanted to go for a walk in the garden but was stopped by the royal courtier who was by the gate at the time and said she couldn't leave the palace. Even though Anastasia insisted on going to the garden, the royal courtier and the guards would not let her go. She realised that there was no way out.

Anastasia returned to her room when the sun began to set. A little later she heard a tap on the window and saw that the white bird was there. She opened the window and the bird started leaping from branch to branch as if walking down invisible stairs. Anastasia realized that it was showing her how to get to the garden using the tree. She followed it, and after a minute she was down, a tall maze of rose bushes rising before her. She boldly stepped into it and heard a horse snorting. In a moment the white horse she had seen the day before stood in front of her, and behind him was the prince of the White Kingdom she had met at the ball. He was tall, dignified and friendly, and he smiled, his horse bowing to her again.

"Glad to see you again, Anastasia," he said, kissing her hand gently.

"Yes… me too, Your Highness," she said timidly.

"Call me Erik. And this is Acorn." The prince glanced playfully at his horse.

"So this beauty is yours... Yesterday I saw him in the garden."

She went to the horse and started stroking him.

"Anastasia, I have to tell you something important," Erik began seriously, and she focused all her attention on him – "You are a remarkable young lady, who is worthy of taking a queen's throne and reigning along a king all her life", Erik stopped for moment, then took a deep breath and continued:

"I have called you here to tell you that the Black Prince is not the one who will give you the opportunity to reign to an old age. He is deadly, and even one of his kisses would kill you."

Anastasia felt a pang piercing her soul and her eyes began to shimmer with tears.

Erik took both her hands in his and fell to his knees.

"I called you because I wanted to tell you one more thing. I want you to be the queen who rules the White Kingdom with me, Anastasia. Be my wife and I will give you my heart and my kingdom."

Anastasia couldn't believe what she was hearing. She began to realize that marrying the Black Prince she had fallen in love with, would lead to her doom. She felt what Erik was saying was true, it explained why she had experienced the unbearable pain in her heart after kissing the Black Prince. Tears of sadness rolled down her cheeks.

"But Erik, why is the Black Prince deadly... and why do you want to marry me?" she asked.

"Because his heart is black and full of poison and will destroy the life of the one he has chosen."

Anastasia started feeling sick and Prince Erik caught her gently and put his white cloak on the ground for her to sit on. She received the worst possible news, that she would lose her life if she married the Black Prince; but at the same time this handsome prince wanted her hand, and that gave her immediate comfort, though her feelings were completely confused.

"Anastasia, as soon as I saw you, I realized that you were the woman I've been waiting to meet my whole life..."

Deeply moved, she looked into his beautiful browns eyes, and saw how warm they were.

"How beautiful are your words, Erik... But how can I avoid my unfortunate destiny to marry the Black Prince?"

"Anastasia, I would take you away immediately, but the Black Prince will chase you until he finds you, so you have to go back to the castle tonight. There's only one way he would let you go - if he forgets he has ever met you."

Anastasia looked at him with great astonishment:

"But how could that happen?"

"The elixir that brings you back to life after the deadly kisses of the Black Prince is the only thing that can wipe you out of his mind," said Erik, "that elixir was prepared many years ago by a wizard who was honoured in the kingdom of the Black Prince. The wizard loved the prince as his son, but the prince's heartlessness drove him away, and no one heard anything about him ever since.

He left behind only this elixir that would save the life of the prince's chosen one, but it is enough for just 7 days.

Only this elixir can erase you from the Black Prince's memory and you will have to make him drink one of the bottles. Then you will be free from him."

It seemed to Anastasia that everything was just a dream. It was a question of life and death, and she was really grateful to Prince Erik for giving her a chance to save herself. She nodded and, deeply in thought, stood up to go back to the palace.

"Acorn will be in the garden every morning at sunrise," Prince Erik continued, "and he will wait for you to come so that he could take you to the White Kingdom where I will be waiting for you."

Anastasia smiled through tears and wished she could meet him again, because that would mean she had a future ahead - a bright and beautiful life which prince Erik was offering to her.

She returned to her room, climbing the tree back and a moment later someone knocked on the door. It was the royal courtier who informed her that dinner was served and the Black Prince was waiting for her in the dining room. She got dressed quickly and went to meet again her magnetic, deadly fiancé.

That evening, Anastasia had no convenient occasion to serve the elixir to the Black Prince and instead, he kissed her again and she experienced the same agony during the night. The same thing was repeated the next day and the day after, though she was carrying a bottle of elixir with her, and was looking out for an opportunity to give it to her fiancé, but she never got a chance. Time was ticking on, and she felt that life was slipping away from her grasp. She had to find a way to make the Black Prince drink the elixir. Six days passed and only one night remained until the wedding, and one last bottle of "*Ambrosiae antidotos*".

In the morning after waking up from another dramatic night, she thought of Prince Erik and a warm sense of hope filled her heart.

The Black Prince was nowhere to be seen during that last day and Anastasia did not know where he could be. She had only one last chance to save her life, and she had to serve him the elixir before he kissed her.

The night came and she joined the Black Prince for the last dinner. Anastasia picked the most beautiful dress from the wardrobe – a sparkling gown that was the colour of the night sky and covered with numerous diamonds sparkling like stars. She looked truly astounding. When she stepped into the hall, the Black Prince stood frozen for a moment, his face full of admiration and passion.

"Anastasia, the hours left till our wedding tomorrow seem to me like an eternity," intoned the

Black Prince," you are absolutely irresistible, and I will not feel peace until I make you mine."

Anastasia swallowed hard and felt as if she couldn't breathe for a moment.

"Let's spend more time together tonight then, and drink a glass of wine on the balcony," she suggested, her heart pounding.

The Black Prince nodded and ordered everyone to leave them alone. Then he stood before her and reached out his hand. Anastasia took it and they went out onto the beautiful terrace.

A servant came silently and brought two glasses of wine, then retired without saying a word. The Black Prince was drinking faster than Anastasia and soon emptied his glass. Still, she managed to pour the little bottle of elixir unnoticed into her glass. She looked into his eyes and felt them calling her. An overpowering attraction was drawing her close to him, and she felt she only wanted to be in his arms. She wanted to taste once more the sweetness of his kisses, to feel his hands touching her. She was desperately in love with him and felt she was ready to surrender, even if that cost her life. She let him wrap his arms around her, and in that last moment when their eyes met, full of passion, Anastasia - almost breathless – put up the glass to his lips... and he took it and sipped.

Anastasia gently caressed his face, and a teardrop fell down her cheek. Then she took the glass from his hand and drank up the remaining wine. At that moment, when they were all alone, driven by the power of a deadly love, they pressed their lips together for the last time.

Would she manage to stay alive, with just a single sip from the elixir? Was this last kiss going to cost her life? The rest of the evening seemed to be clouded by a fog, and Anastasia got lost in this unimaginable, secret world the Black Prince's eyes were summoning her to.

The morning rays lit up the terrace and woke Anastasia, who seemed to have no idea where she was and why she was there. She saw the beautiful colours of the upcoming spring, and heard the neighing of a horse nearby. It was Acorn, who was waiting for her in the garden, and Anastasia, as if still in a daze, went to her room and climbed onto the tree. As she descended, she remembered the day when the Black Prince was brought to her, wounded, and how she healed him with her herbs. How little by little they got closer and how he had chosen her to become his wife. Everything seemed like a fairy tale in which she had fallen in love with the enchanted prince. Her story with the Black Prince didn't have a happy endling, but she was safe now and ready for a new beginning. In her heart she felt joy mixed with pain. Pain, because she was leaving behind the one she had fallen in love with, but also joy, because a new love awaited her that would bring her happiness.

Anastasia reached the garden and climbed onto Acorn, who would take her to the White Kingdom where Prince Erik was waiting for her.

The Fairy

Everyone knows that fairies are beautiful and gentle creatures who fulfil wishes and help people. Little is known, however, about their life. When a fairy appears to an unhappy person in need of help and asks what their wish is, the person is so happy that they don't even wonder if the fairy has her own desires or needs help. Because, in fact, fairies have no right to fulfil their own wishes, but only to help people. Yet, they would be very happy if someone asked them how their day was or offered them a cup of tea.

In the country of the fairies, there lived a comparatively plain-looking fairy named Bluebell. She was neither elegant nor exquisite. Other fairies considered her eccentric, because her clothing was made of leaves and flowers while they were dressed in silk and stardust. She didn't like spending much time in the magic room with the other fairies who coloured their garments, braided their hair, or talked about beautiful gins in distant lands.

Bluebell lived in the suburbs of Fairy Land in a small old house. When it rained, the whole house was flooded and so, sometimes when she appeared in front of a person who wanted to make a wish, she was sneezing or had her clothes soaking wet, and she didn't look especially magical. But actually, there was something very special about this plain and modest fairy – her really good heart. She liked to help people, and then she observed them secretly to see if anyone whose wish she had fulfilled was going down a bad track. In that case, Bluebell sent them small obstacles to remind them that they must always be good. Every time she made a person's desire come true, in the end, the fairy told them this: "And remember – always be kind."

She loved nature and her most beloved friends were the forest trees and plants where she drew strength from. She loved the warm hugs of the trees that stretched their branches towards her and gently embraced her. The short grass blades hopped excitedly when they saw her and waited for her to caress them.

Bluebell stayed in her little house and scanned the Book of desires. All fairies had this book, the pages of which were blank, but when a fairy opened it, various pictures appeared there, pictures out of the lives of people who wished for something or needed help. When Bluebell turned a page, she could see pictures of an unfortunate child in torn clothes, sitting in front of the fire, stretching out his frozen hands. Or, a bankrupt merchant who had no food to take home to his big family. She quickly went to help with her magic wand.

Bluebell also saw pictures of a little bunny or a deer, who had lost their parents, and helped them find their way home.

One night, going through the pages of the book, Bluebell saw the picture of a young man, sitting alone by a lake, looking sad, throwing small stones in it. Below the picture, it was written: "I want to be free to choose my own destiny." Bluebell did not know why the young man was so sad and what his wish meant, so she put on the clothes that made her invisible and went to the lake. She wanted to know what the young man's story was.

The young lad heard a rustle in the bushes and turned to see who was there, but he saw no one, and continued to throw pebbles in the pond, sighing heavily. Bluebell followed him as he left and saw that he headed to the castle. She soon realised that the young man was Prince Jared, the King's son, the same one who was going to get married in a month and the king was preparing a great and glorious wedding for him.

Bluebell went to his room and sprinkled some magical dust over the prince's pillow. Once he had spent one night sleeping on it, Bluebell would collect the magic powder, put it in a seashell and hear its story about the Prince's dreams and thoughts. This way she would know his heart's desire.

Two years ago, the King had organised a flamboyant ball to honour the beautiful Princess Flavia, who had come to his kingdom from a distant land. There, Prince Jared had met her for the first time, and a few weeks later, they were already engaged. The prince was impressed by her beauty, but when the two began to spend more time together, he found out that the princess had a cruel heart. She liked to humiliate people who didn't follow her whims. The prince had a good heart and treated his subjects with kindness.

The Princess's maid was a tender girl whose name was Blossom. She was always close to the princess, and she suffered most from her bad temper. Blossom was gentle and vulnerable, and Prince Jared noticed how unfair her mistress was treating her. One day, the princess dropped a cup of tea on the floor and Blossom bent to clean the mess. The princess slapped her face, accusing her of clumsiness. Prince Jared saw how unfair the princess was to blame the poor girl and saw tears in Blossom's eyes. He felt sorry for her and later on tried to talk the princess into being more considerate to her servants. Princess Flavia didn't like that conversation and retreated to her quarters.

Gradually, Prince Jared's heart began to sway away from her and got increasingly attached to Blossom, who was always so kind and defenceless.

It was only a month until the wedding, when Princess Flavia, Prince Jared, and a few ladies and gentlemen were walking around the gardens of the palace. Blossom followed the princess, who just then broke the heel of her shoe. The maid gave the princess her coat to sit on and her own shoes so that she could continue her walk and bended down to help her put them on. Princess Flavia looked at her haughtily:

"What a clumsy creature you are," she said as she pushed Blossom backward. "Do not touch my leg with your dirty hands. It's enough that I have to wear your nasty shoes."

Prince Jared couldn't stand watching Blossom being humiliated, but he could do nothing in front of the courtiers. He sighed quietly and turned his head away from the princess.

Later that evening, when the princess went to bed, and Blossom was alone in the garden, Prince Jared came out dressed in a dark mantle, so none of the servants could recognise him, and went secretly to meet Blossom.

She was sitting on a bench, staring thoughtfully at the moon as he approached her and asked her:

"Do you mind if I sat alongside you?"

Blossom looked at him, a little frightened.

"Do not worry, I'm Jared, I won't do you any harm," he said in a soothing voice.

"All right, Prince Jared, you may sit here, and I have to go back to my room," she said, and began to rise, but Prince Jared took her hand to stop her.

"Please stay here to keep me company," he said while looking at her tenderly.

They sat side by side in the quiet summer night.

"Do you like watching the stars in the sky?" he asked.

"Yes, it is very beautiful and peaceful," said Blossom, "there are so many stars in the sky that sparkle and decorate the night. Sometimes I wish I were a star too," she said in a trembling voice.

Prince Jared felt a strong desire to hug her, and gently touched her hand. Blossom looked at him in fear.

"Can I trust you with something, Blossom?" he asked.

"Yes, of course, Prince Jared. But I don't think I'm worthy of being in your company and talking to you." Blossom dropped her eyes.

Prince Jared fell on his knees in front of her and lifted her chin.

"Blossom, I know how difficult it is for you and how hard you suffer," he began," I know you have a good heart and you are so beautiful…"

"The Princess is far more beautiful than me, Prince Jared, I'm just an ordinary girl."

"No, Blossom, you are not an ordinary girl. The real beauty comes from inside, and you are beautiful inside and out," Jared gently took her hands, "What I wanted to tell you is that I'm not in love with the princess and I don't want to marry her. I want to marry you."

Blossom looked at him, shocked. It was the last thing she had expected to hear, and she could not believe her ears.

"I don't know what to say, Prince Jared," she barely uttered.

"Let's escape together. We will get married secretly, live in a small house and have children, " he said excitedly," I want to take care for you, my sweet girl, and to be happy together with you."

Blossom didn't know what to answer. She had noticed that Prince Jared treated everyone well, and that sometimes he even secretly helped his servants with their work. She liked him and admired him, but she never allowed her heart to fall for him, that royalty who would soon marry her mistress. But on that starry night, she felt as if she was in a beautiful fairy tale, where the dreams that she didn't allow herself to dream of, became reality.

"Prince Jared, what will happen to you if you run away with me and someone recognises you?" wondered Blossom.

"Call me Jared, dear Blossom. I am a human, just like you. Fate decided that I was born in a royal family, but my heart chose to love a common girl. I will follow my heart. My father has other sons who will inherit the throne."

"But they are not like you, Prince Jared." She paused for a moment, "Forgive me, Jared, I mean – they behave like young masters, they are not kind like you."

"My brother Philip will be a good king," Jared said. Then he suddenly heard footsteps. "Come with me quickly," he said, grabbing Blossom by the hand and pulling her behind a bush.

"There is somebody here, keep quiet," Jared said, embracing Blossom as he covered her with his mantle. She could smell his pleasant odour, was this real or was it just a dream?

Prince Jared looked deeply in her eyes and gently caressed her face.

"You will be my lovely wife, dear Blossom," he said, "I want to spend my life with you. Wait for me tomorrow at the same place, do not carry any luggage. Together we will escape. There is a place we can stay and someone who will hide us."

Blossom started to go, but then stopped, turned to him and asked,

"Do you really love me, Jared?"

"With all my heart and soul, Blossom," he said and smiled.

"Then I will love you with every part of me," she declared, and a tear tore away from her eye and went down her cheek.

Late at night, long after Prince Jared returned to his room, somebody knocked at the door. It was the royal counsellor. He went into the Prince's room and said he had some confidential news.

"Your highness," the counsellor began, "tonight you were on a walk in the garden if I am not mistaken…" He looked at him seriously from beneath his eyebrows.

"I'm not sure what you mean by this, sir?" said the prince and sat in the chair, leaning against its back.

"Your highness knows that the wedding is to take place next month, which is important to the whole kingdom and which is your duty to your father and your ancestors," the royal counsellor continued in a solemn voice.

"I'm sure my father and my ancestors would like me to be happy, despite my duty," the prince said and looked with determination in the royal counsellor's eyes.

"You will inevitably be happy with a beautiful wife like the princess."

The counsellor approached the prince and in a quieter voice spoke:

"I hope you understand that all safety measures have already been taken and the princess will expect a new maid tomorrow to come."

Prince Jared rose from his chair, he felt as if a flash of lightning pierced him.

"What have you done to Blossom?" he shouted, and grabbed the counsellor by the shoulders. "Where is Blossom?"

"The princess's maid will be absolutely safe if the prince fulfils his duty and gets married to the noble princess as it's been planned."

Prince Jared was shocked. He went out onto the balcony and looked to the garden. He passed his fingers through his hair and sighed heavily.

"Take me to see Blossom," the prince said.

"Your highness can see the Princess's maid for the last time, if you promise you will not resist the wedding."

"I'll do whatever it takes to protect Blossom."

The royal adviser said he would take the Prince to Blossom the following night, after the Prince accompanied Princess Flavia to a palace ball organised in honour of the newly arrived guests from distant kingdoms.

That night was very hard for the prince, he went to bed but he couldn't sleep. He lay down, thinking how he could still avoid the wedding with the heartless princess and escape with Blossom. But no matter how much he thought, he couldn't find a way.

The next day it seemed to him as if time had stopped, hours dragged like days. Prince Jared accompanied princess Flavia to the ball and everything there seemed so vain and blurry to him. He could barely wait for the night to come so he could see Blossom.

The royal counsellor knocked on the door, and Prince Jared leaped from his chair and opened it. The two of them went to the dungeon, and the counsellor opened a door to a secret passage that led them to a second door and a small room. Light in it was scarce, but it was warm and clean. Prince Jared had heard that there was such a place in the palace, where people who threatened the royal family were held, but he had never been here before.

He saw Blossom, who was sitting in an armchair, hiding her face in her palms. He went to her and hugged her tightly.

"Blossom, I'm so sorry," said Jared, gently caressing her shoulders. "Someone saw us when we met the night before in the garden, and now we're both in danger. But I will not allow anything bad to happen to you and I will do whatever it takes so that you are well."

"Jared, I was so worried. I did not know what was going to happen to me," Blossom said through tears.

"You didn't do anything wrong, Blossom. I give you my word that you will be safe."

Jared didn't know how to tell her that he would have to marry the princess to save the one he loved.

"Dear Blossom, if I can't come to you when you leave the kingdom," Jared's voice trembled with feeling, "please live happily and be free."

He caressed her face once more and walked away.

And it was on the next day, when the Prince went by the lake and made a wish to be with Blossom, no matter how impossible that seemed.

Bluebell heard the prince's story from the shell and the magical dust from the prince's pillow, and her good heart was very moved. She wanted to make his wish come true immediately, so she took out her magic wand, and said some magic and mysterious words, which would make all the obstacles between Blossom and Prince Jared disappear. Then she quickly started turning the pages of the Book of desires to see if under the prince's painting appeared the words: "The desire was fulfilled," but for her great surprise there was nothing there. It could mean only one thing, someone else had made a wish that was the opposite of that of the prince, and she had to find out what that wish was.

She had just one choice, although what she was about to do was forbidden – she had to go to the Mystery house where they got the magic wands, wish books, invisible clothes, magical shoes, fairy dust and all other magic stuff. In the centre of the Mystery house, there was a garden of flowers. Each flower was someone's desire. Bluebell slipped into the garden in her invisible clothes and hurried to find Prince Jared's flower. Next to it, she saw another flower that was planted in the garden before that of the prince. Bluebell bent down and listened to its quiet whisper. The flower whispered, "I wish to get Prince Jared as a gift for my birthday, and that he would be my obedient servant for the rest of his days."

Bluebell realised that this wish was made by Princess Flavia, and she frowned, knowing that this was not the desire of a loving heart, but a whim of a spoiled princess accustomed to receiving whatever she wanted.

She quietly walked out of the garden, looking back over her shoulder to check if anyone had spotted her. And then she heard the footsteps of Misses Tulip, the director of the Mystery house. Her gait could not be mistaken, for she had to take ten steps where an ordinary fairy made just one. Bluebell hurriedly put on the invisible cloak and managed to pass her by unnoticed, then went directly to the palace. There she saw the princess, who was picking up roses from the garden and then removing their petals one by one.

No fairy was allowed to appear before a human being who was entrusted to another fairy, so Bluebell could not show herself to the princess and talk to her directly. Instead, she summoned the wind to help her. It started blowing and lifted the petals of the roses from the ground, then arranged them in the form of a face – an image of a girl who reminded the princess of her maid Blossom. She got scared when she saw this, and fled to the palace. She knew Blossom had been sent away for some reason, and she did not care what had happened to her, though they had grown up together. To her, Blossom was just an insignificant maid.

Prince Jared went to the garden late in the evening. He was walking alone and sighing heavily when he heard some soft whisper from the nearby tree:

"Psst, Prince Jared, come here."

Prince Jared approached the tree and saw Bluebell's dazed face. He was surprised when he saw this strange figure, dressed in different leaves and wearing large flower-shaped shoes, who held a glowing stick in her hand.

"Who are you?" he asked.

"I'm Bluebell. I come from the County of Fairies to help you."

It was the first time Prince Jared saw a fairy in his life, and he was amazed by her cheerfulness and the fresh and fragrant smell of flowers coming from her.

Bluebell told him how she knew about his desire and his love for Blossom, but also that she can't fulfil his wish unless the princess gave up hers.

"I have a very special gift for you. This is a ring made of the rays of the sun that makes anyone who wears it look beautiful and radiant. Use it carefully."

After this brief meeting, Bluebell put the invisible cloak on and vanished in front of Prince Jared's eyes, leaving him even more thoughtful than he was before that.

The next day, he went to have breakfast with the princess. She was sitting at the other end of the table. Prince Jared asked the servants to leave them alone and turned to her:

"Princess Flavia, can I ask you a question?" he began.

"Tell me what it is, Prince Jared," she said without much interest.

"Why do you want to marry me?"

The princess looked at him puzzled then continued to eat without saying anything. Prince Jared felt embarrassed by her silence, and stood up to go. Before he left, the princess said:

"Prince Jared, the most important thing about a couple is that they look good together. You are handsome and I can be completely beautiful when we are together."

Prince Jared didn't expect such an answer. But knowing how little interest the princess had in other people, and with what great care she tended to herself, he realised she was telling the truth. An idea occurred to him that he decided to put into action as soon as possible.

"Princess Flavia, please do me the honour of meeting me on the balcony overlooking the garden, where you and I will be able to discuss a matter that I think will be very interesting to you."

Princess Flavia nodded her head in agreement.

Later that evening, Prince Jared waited for Princess Flavia on the beautiful porch, its columns wrapped in ivy. It was a delightful night, fireflies flew in the distance, and the stars shone really bright. Princess Flavia walked slowly dressed in a long evening gown. She came to Prince Jared.

"You look charming as ever," Prince Jared said, bowing slightly.

"Thank you," she answered confidently.

"You and I, Princess Flavia, have similar backgrounds," he began, sipping a little wine, "but I think it is more important to have similar ideals and dreams."

Flavia stared at him.

"You, Princess Flavia, want to be always beautiful and that's your wish. You don't need me for that," Prince Jared stared at her resolutely. "You know, I have something that could be yours if you fulfilled my wish."

And then Prince Jared pulled out of his pocket the ring made out of sun rays. It started glowing, and Princess Flavia looked at it admiringly and reached out to take it, but Prince Jared put it back in his pocket.

"What is this ring? It must be a gift for me. Give it to me," Flavia demanded.

"This ring makes the person wearing it look beautiful beyond comparison. You can have it if you denounce your wish to marry me."

"But I don't want to give up my wish. Give me this ring," Princess Flavia said, irritated.

"Princess Flavia, you don't love me, and you won't be happy with me. But this ring will give you what you really want – you will always shine."

Princess Flavia looked at him angrily and left Prince Jared alone on the balcony. He sighed heavily. This was his last chance, it had to work.

Meanwhile, Bluebell went secretly to Blossom who was still locked alone in the secret cell in the palace. The room was dark, there was only one candle lit, she was sitting on a chair, her elbows on the table and her head buried in her hands. And then, she noticed some kind of green light approaching, like hundreds of fireflies flying towards her. She lifted her head in surprise and stood up from the chair. Then she felt someone stepping on her foot.

"Oh, I am very sorry," Bluebell said, shaking her magic wand, which lit up so brightly that the whole room started glowing in green. "I didn't mean to step on your foot." Bluebell put the magic wand in a vase of withered flowers that was on the table, and the flowers immediately revived and blossomed.

"But who are you?" asked the perplexed Blossom.

Bluebell caressed the girl's hand and looked at her warmly.

"I am a fairy who has come to visit you at this difficult time."

Bluebell swung around and started humming a cheerful melody, and an ivy appeared and started growing on the walls; soft grass covered the rough stone floor, and in the corners of the room, beautiful flowers blossomed.

The girl was astonished when she saw the room transform into a marvellous garden.

Then Bluebell said not to worry too much, and that somehow things would be fine in the end. She gave her a strawberry toast to eat and a glass of elderberry juice to drink.

"I will be nearby, and I won't allow anything bad to happen to you, dear child," Bluebell said before leaving. Then she made a bed of lilies for Blossom to sleep in:

"You must be very tired, dear. Go to bed and restore your strength after I leave. I will come to you again."

Blossom felt consoled, knowing that she wasn't alone anymore. The bed of lilies and the room that had turned into a flower garden were the most amazing things she had ever seen. She lay down on the fragrant flowers and slept peacefully the whole night.

Meanwhile, preparation for the wedding was at its peak, and time was ticking away. Princess Flavia was always sullen and didn't want to talk to anyone. She spent more and more time dressing up herself and was always in a bad mood.

The evening before the wedding, Prince Jared sat alone in the throne hall where the ceremony was going to be held. He took out the ring made of sun rays, looked at it carefully and put it on his finger, without knowing that he was being observed by Princess Flavia, who had hid herself behind a column. Princess Flavia was amazed when she saw how the prince's appearance changed and he started shining and looking amazingly handsome. After that, he took the ring off and put it in his pocket.

That night Princess Flavia couldn't sleep well, not because her wedding was the next day, but because she wanted this ring more than anything else.

So, early in the morning, she got dressed and sent her servants to call Prince Jared.

Not long after, he knocked on the door.

"Come in," she said in a harsh tone.

"You asked to see me," Prince Jared looked tired and sad.

"That's right, Prince Jared," she said, and got up from the chair. She went to the window, "I want you to give me the ring. I denounce my wish, I won't marry you."

Prince Jared was amazed to hear these words. He went to her, took her hand and gently kissed it, then put the ring in her palm.

"Princess Flavia," he said excitedly, "I'm so glad you made that decision. Here's the ring that intrigued you so much. I hope it brings you happiness."

She took the ring, put it on her finger and looked into the mirror. A smile appeared on her face for the first time, for she saw herself in full brilliance as she had always wanted.

Bluebell was in her house when she noticed that one of the pages of the Book of desires started shining. She opened the book and saw a picture of a young man who was standing in the palace garden dressed in festive clothes. Below the picture, she saw the words: "I wish to marry Blossom on this sunny summer day."

Bluebell jumped with joy, then took her magic wand and a basket full of presents – they were small, the size of a matchbox but, when opened, turned into beautiful hats, china dinnerware and tea sets, golden jewellery, luxurious gloves, all kinds of surprises for every guest who would attend the wedding and all the people from the nearby villages.

Blossom woke up from the sound of someone unlocking her cell-door. She was startled when she saw it was the prison guard. Behind him was Prince Jared, who was dressed in white clothes and looked very happy.

"Dear Blossom," he began, and fell to his knees. "I was hoping that day would come and I would have the honour of offering you to bind your life to mine."

Blossom felt her body trembling with the chills of excitement.

"That day is finally here, and I want to ask you to become my wife," Prince Jared picked a small flower from the garden, made a ring out of it and put it on her finger.

Blossom's eyes filled with tears, and she shook her head in agreement, then Prince Jared hugged her tightly and picked her in his arms.

At this wonderful and jubilant moment, Bluebell appeared very excited.

"My dear children," she said, "today is such a beautiful day, when a heartfelt desire interweaves the lives of two innocent youths." And then she took matters in her hands.

Prince Jared withdrew to wait for Blossom in the throne hall. Bluebell changed the girl in an exquisite dress, beautiful as a white rose, and put on her head a crown of white flowers.

When the guests gathered in anticipation of the new royal couple, they were surprised to see that along the prince was walking not Princess Flavia but her maid. The girl looked innocent and beautiful, so everyone present agreed that she was undoubtedly a maiden who deserved the Prince's love.

Bluebell was so happy that her eyes filled with tears, which started dripping down her cheeks and to the ground where they turned into flowers.

Prince Jared and Princess Blossom lived happily ever after. They reigned for many years and were always good and fair to all of their subjects.

Inner beauty is the sun, which illuminates the souls and penetrates the depths where darkness reigns. Love is the power that warms even the coldest hearts. Thus, the love of Prince Jared and Blossom illuminated the lives of many people from near and far.

The Journey

Thoughts thumped in my head, a hurricane of different thoughts changing so fast, and all led me to the idea that I had to go on a journey that would lead me to my destiny.

I had dreamt about him, a man whose image I saw clearly. In the beginning, it was like I was seeing him under water, just a vague silhouette. But after appearing in my dreams through hundreds of nights, his image became more lucid and I saw it quite clearly. The face of a young man, nice, attractive. I woke up in the morning and felt an indescribably strong attraction pulling me towards him. I had never met him in reality, I could only see him in my dreams.

I've always been different from the others. During our children's games, I was pretending to be a leader of an Indian tribe, with a bow and arrows in my hand, who led her Indians to discover new lands. I climbed high trees and observed the life of the bugs in the meadow in front of our house while other girls played princesses, dressing up in their mother's clothes. I didn't go dancing on Friday night, I went to the field to shoot with my bow. As I grew up, I was too busy reading books, and I didn't pay attention to Richard, who was following me when I was back in school, nor to Daniel, who left flowers at my door every Sunday afternoon and then hurried away because he was too shy. The other girls commented on how absent-minded I always was, and how I never noticed anything except for the books, I had buried my nose in.

My childhood days passed like a happy laugh that lasted so briefly.

As if yesterday I was a child, and now I was all grown up – a girl in the prime of my youth. Yet I felt some unexplainable absence, like something was missing. And I also had the feeling that my fate would be different from that of other people, that an adventure was waiting for me, an adventure far beyond the horizons reached by everyone else. Looking at the night sky, I saw a bright star that blinked only when I looked at it and no one else noticed that. I wondered if this star sent me the dreams of this mysterious man.

One night, when I saw him again in my sleep, he smiled as if he was calling me with his gaze. He was standing close to me, but when I reached out to touch him, he wasn't there. He was far away, almost out of touch. I saw a long road lying between us and he was there, at the end of it.

When I woke up from this dream, I understood the message that was sent to me – I had to find this man. He was the missing piece of me.

One morning, I woke up and gathered a bunch of clothes, a bottle of water, a small cooking pot, my grandmother's big blanket, and a little food. I hid the money I had, under my clothes, to pay for shelter for the night and food, and took my bow and arrows to use them in case of danger.

That's how I started my epic journey. Adventure into the unknown, during which I was going to be overthrown by storms and lifted up by rising suns. A road full of thorns, stones and barriers. But this time, it would lead me to the place where the missing part of my heart was.

I got out of the town, where I had grown up, and left behind my childhood. A long way was waiting for me and I had to behave like a grown up girl with the courage to face every challenge.

When the sun started its way down the horizon, I had already reached the border of the area. I looked behind me and saw how small the city I had grown in looked like. There was a wide field ahead of me, and somewhere in the distance, I could hear a bird singing. I spread my grandmother's blanket, which was warm and large enough for two people, and I wrapped myself in it. It was cosy and pleasant, the stars gleamed beautifully, and somewhere near me, a cricket was playing a concert that lulled me in a sweet dream.

There, somewhere far away, I saw him – the handsome young man who was waiting for me. I wanted to ask him whether he was also walking towards me, but at that moment, a gentle touch woke me up. A wheatear caressed my cheek and tickled me. I rubbed my eyes and looked at the horizon.

The wheat field was so vast that it was only after I had walked for two days and spent the night in the wheat, that a wide forest was revealed in front of me. Beautiful trees stood dignified, waving their branches as if they were caressing the wind. I felt it in my hair, a scent of freshness, and then I felt the thrill from my dream, the wind reminded me of the man I was looking for.

The forest was a completely unknown place for me, but I hoped that there would be no danger. My bow and arrows were at hand and they gave me courage. The forest was spacious and bright during the day, the sun painted different patterns on the forest carpet. I was walking almost without rest. The food I had taken with me was almost over, but I managed to find wild berries that were sweet and refreshing.

As darkness fell, I started hearing different sounds from near and far, and they startled me. Everything sank into darkness, and the trees became huge statues, as if created to intimidate. I carried two small candles and pebbles to kindle them with. I stopped by a tree and lit one of the candles. And then I saw something moving near the tree.

Chills ran through my body, but I gathered the courage to bring the candle closer and see what was hiding there. In the dim light, I saw a little fluffy face and two scared black eyes. It was a strange forest creature, the kind I had never seen before. It looked like a bunny, but it didn't have long ears, and was twice as big as a cat. Its fur was very soft and light of colour. I stretched out my hand to caress it, and it was petrified, I could see it slightly shuddering. I took out a bunch of blueberries I had left and brought them under the tiny nose of the fluffy creature. It stopped trembling and ate the blueberries. Then it allowed me to caress it. So, in this dark night, I found an unexpected friend. I called it Fluffy.

I spread out my big blanket and lay down, nestling the fluffy little creature close to my heart. It felt so cosy. I was very tired after the long walk that I fell asleep instantly and my dream was very sweet.

The morning sun smiled at me and brushed my face with its rays, inviting me to get up. The trees were alive again, bathed in the light, and the little creature was still cuddled close to me, sleeping. I started to caress it and it opened its eyes. They were stunning colours, a mixture of blue and black. This little creature radiated goodness and there wasn't any aggression in it, so I loved it with all my heart. Though it was an animal, and I was a human, I asked it if it would like to join me for my journey. Its eyes filled with joy, and it willingly came with me.

So, Fluffy and I walked together through the woods. During the day, while we were walking, I found chestnuts and cooked them in the small cooking pot I carried with me. Fluffy watched me curiously while I lit the fire. After the chestnuts were ready, we swallowed them so quickly, that I had to go looking for more in the woods for us two gluttons.

The journey through the forest with my cuddly friend brought me very happy days, and warm and cosy nights.

When we reached the end of the forest, I saw a long path before us. I looked in the distance, but there was nothing except this path, which stretched to the horizon. I turned to my little friend and smiled. I motioned Fluffy to go forward, but it didn't move from its place. When I leaned over to caress it, I read in its eyes that it couldn't continue going with me. I understood that the forest was its home. I was sad because I wanted to keep it forever with me, but I couldn't. I hugged Fluffy once more, and it touched my face with its paw. I made a wish to see Fluffy again.

I couldn't stay long, my food was almost over, and in a day's time, I had to find food supplies from somewhere. I took a few steps forward, but turned to look at the fluffy creature. It looked at me with sad eyes, and a few tears fell of mine.

The path I continued on was long and sandy. My feet were sinking in the sand and it was very tiring to walk, but I couldn't rest for long. When it got dark, I hadn't seen anything else on the horizon yet. The night was cold and a strong wind was blowing from all sides. In a crazy dance, the sand twirled around, hitting me and blurring my eyes. It was so cold, the wind was penetrating under the blanket, and I was trembling, but I couldn't find shelter anywhere. I couldn't fall asleep and felt so lonely. I hid my face in my hands and waited for the wind to stop.

I don't remember falling asleep, but after that cold night, I was woken up by a sunny morning. I stood up and shook off the sand of my clothes and hair, then walked down the desert road. I walked for another day and at the end of the evening, when it was dark, I saw a small inn in the distance. I reached it and when I entered, I asked the owners for a small room to spend the night in and paid with the money I had taken with me.

The room in this inn was really narrow. There was a tiny bed and a table with a chunk of bread and a piece of cheese, and beside them a jar of water. I was so hungry that this piece of bread with cheese seemed to me the most delicious food in the world. After I ate, I went to sleep. I slept in bed after such a long time and as soon as I closed my eyes, I fell asleep. In my dream that night, I was sitting in a garden, deep in thought. My feet were immersed in a small stream. And then he came again, he touched my shoulder, and when I turned around, I saw his face up close. His eyes were so beautiful, and I saw softness and kindness in them. He invited me to dance, but I was surprised how could we dance without music? He looked at me with a smile and said that music was in our hearts, where love was hidden. Then he took me by the hand and we danced in the small stream with bare feet. It was so cheerful.

When I asked him what his name was, I suddenly was woken up by the songs of a bird that was not just singing but screaming at my window! What an insolent creature to pull me out of this beautiful dream with its squeaky voice. But the bird continued screaming and even started to hurl itself at the window. It was very strange and aroused anxiety in me. I decided to get ready and leave the inn as fast as I could. I washed my face and put the rest of the bread and cheese in my bundle. I walked quietly out of the house and when I reached a tree not far from it, I hid behind it and looked back. Then I saw a man searching my room, looking for someone, probably me. I didn't know who he was and why he was looking for me, but I realised that this bird had protected me from danger. I looked up to thank it, but I didn't see it.

I continued my way. The sun was bright, it was hot and my mouth got dry, and I wasn't able to fill my water bottle in the morning. I walked for hours, but I couldn't find water anywhere. I was already starting to feel dizzy when the same bird that woke me up in the morning began to fly beside me. It was carrying a bunch of grapes in its beak. I stretched out my arms and it dropped the delicious fruit in my palms. I thanked it for protecting me from danger in the morning and coming to my rescue again. Then, I sat down to rest and to eat the grapes. The bird stayed near me while I was eating. When I got up to continue my way, the bird nodded and flew away. It looked back to me and I felt it was showing me the right direction to go and I followed it until I lost the bird from my sight.

The days passed like autumn leaves falling one by one from a tree. My long journey was exhausting me and I often felt lonely. At times when fatigue prevailed, I was wondering if the man from my dreams wasn't just a fantasy. Did he really exist?

I don't remember how much time has passed. I continued my way as if to the end of the world and then I reached a wide area, all covered with soft grass. I really enjoyed walking barefoot on it. At the end of this area, a wilderness began, and wherever I looked, I now saw only empty space with just a few dry trees scattered through the bare land. I decided to sit on the soft grass before I entered the desert. I heard the sound of a horn somewhere in the distance and listened. Encountering strangers in the middle of the desert was too dangerous. I saw a big tree nearby and I decided to climb as high as I could in its crown. I heard the sound of a horn again, but this time closer. Not long after, I heard hooves thudding, and in the distance from the green meadow came men and women with belligerent faces, riding horses. As they approached the desert, I was amazed to see that they weren't people, but centaurs. I had heard stories about them, but I had never seen them live, and I was very excited. But I didn't know if they were friendly, so I was ready to use my bow. They were carrying large bundles with different things wrapped in them – corn, hay, and berries. When they reached the border between the green land and the wilderness, they left all the food and blew the horns again.

After staying there for a very short time, they turned and left. There was a small centaur with a childish face. He was the only one who turned around and looked me straight into the eyes. I was well hidden behind the branches and leaves, but he had somehow noticed me. After all of them left, I climbed down and then I felt something strange about the desert, which kept me from going forward. The day was so beautiful and the sun was so hot, that I decided to lay down and take a nap. I had barely opened my eyes when I saw that I was not alone. The small centaur sat beside me, holding a wooden figurine in his hands, whittling the wood. I was startled and reached for my bow, then directed it towards the centaur.

"Who are you and what do you want from me?" I said, looking at him tentatively.

The centaur left the figurine on the ground, looked at me and said,

"I came to warn you to steer away of the little goblins that live in the wilderness. I cut this figure to show you what they look like."

I looked at the figurine:

"So you come in peace?" I wasn't so worried any longer by the presence of the stranger.

"I come with friendly intentions. What is your name?" he asked me.

I put down the bow and smiled. He smiled back.

"I am Agnes, and what's your name? You look much younger than the other centaurs?"

"I am Fornex, the son of Goghel, the king of our people."

"What kind of people are you? What land do you live in?"

"We are the only remaining centaurs that inhabit the land to the east of the North Sea, up to this area that has been ravaged by the goblins. And this land was once inhabited by us, but the goblins settled underground and devastated it."

"How did they devastate the land," I asked, feeling fear in myself.

"Goblins are omnivorous beings who wipe out everything they see in front of them. We call them 'the invisible enemy', because they dig tunnels underground, devour the roots of plants and trees, and when they are done with them, they eat the animals and the people who live above the ground."

"That's terrifying!" I exclaimed while shivering in horror, "But how do you manage to keep them away from your remaining territory?"

"Our people have managed to capture the goblin's king and hold him hostage. Without him, goblins are disoriented and do not know where to go. Every month, our people carry food at the border to keep the goblins under control."

"How will I cross this desert since there is such a danger?" I said terrified.

"There is a secret passage that only we, the centaurs know, and I can lead you beyond the wilderness through it."

I was very happy to hear that, but I was still worried about crossing the territory of such bloodthirsty creatures.

"If you spend the night here, near this tree, you will be safe," continued Fornex, "I will come back before the sun rises, and I will lead you through the passage."

I nodded and agreed with his plan to meet at dawn.

I could not sleep that night. The weather was warm, the grass beneath the tree, soft and comfortable, but the thought that these terrible goblins were just below me underground didn't allow me peace. I was thinking about my friend Fluffy and the nice time we had together, about the beautiful meadows we crossed and the hills covered with flowers and ivy. I was thinking about the bird that had saved my life and about the fact that all this time I didn't have to use my bow even once. I was thinking about the man from my dreams. As the sun began to emerge on the horizon, my eyes closed. But it was too late to sleep, Fornex would be arriving soon.

In just a little while, I saw him coming, but he wasn't alone. I stood up, folded my blanket, plucked an apple from the tree, and started eating it while Fornex and the other centaur approached. When they got near, I saw that it was a girl. She smiled friendly, but Fornex was serious.

"Morning Agnes," Fornex began, "I hope you've gotten a good night's sleep because we have a long way to go."

"I haven't slept all night, but somehow I will endure. I see we have company," I looked at the smiling centaur girl.

"I'm Megan, it's nice to meet you." She reached out and we shook hands.

"Megan is my sister," Fornex explained with a frowny face, "she saw that I was getting out of the village and said that if I didn't take her with me, she would tell my father that I was gone."

Fornex frowned even more.

We talked for a while and after Megan promised not to bring us any trouble on our way, we headed towards the tunnel.

"How old are you, Megan?" I asked her.

"I'm 35," she said, and smiled even more broadly.

"35 Centaur years are equivalent to 15 human," said Fornex, "I'm 15 centaur years older than her, that's 22 human years or almost 51 centaur years."

The presence of these two new friends brought me a pleasant feeling, as if I wasn't alone on my journey. At times when I needed help, my guiding star sent me helpers that made me feel safe.

Fornex led us to a part of the green meadow, where the grass was a little shorter and paler and an old tree without leaves was standing. He told us to stay close beside him and hit an uneven part of the trunk. At that time, the part of the lawn with the shorter and paler grass we stood on began to descend. Unexpectedly, the further we went, the brighter it became. The light had a greenish hue. When we finally reached the bottom, we saw a wide green path ahead of us, with tall trees on both sides, covered with moss. There was moss on the ground too, as if a soft carpet was spread before us. My concerns were replaced by a nice feeling, I took off my shoes and walked barefoot on the green moss.

The walk through the passage was very pleasant. All along the way, I talked with Fornex and Megan, they told me about how their people settled on these lands that were deserted and they planted fruit trees everywhere. They also told me that all centaurs were great musicians and artists and that each of them had a gift – be it painting, writing poems, or playing a musical instrument.

"What's your gift, Fornex?" I asked.

"I'm composing music," he replied.

"And your talent, Megan?"

"I can sing well," she smiled, and I asked her to sing a song composed by Fornex.

She started singing a beautiful song about a nightingale locked in a golden cage that sang so well that its master gave it its freedom.

The walk through the passage was so pleasant that I forgot about the presence of the goblins somewhere near us. But suddenly, I was startled by a low rumbling sound, and Fornex shouted:

"Run, Agnes, fast, get on Megan's back, and I'll cover you!"

Before I could figure out what was going on, a few goblins came from a hole somewhere on the side and saw us. They run very fast and if it wasn't for Megan and Fornex and their quick hooves, we wouldn't be able to get away.

As we approached the end of the tunnel, and I started to say goodbye to my dear friends, a goblin suddenly popped out from behind and almost grabbed me, but I turned and shot an arrow in his leg.

"Hurry, Agnes, you have to get out of here," Fornex urged.

"But what about you?" I looked at them, frightened.

"We are faster than them and we can get out of the tunnel before they catch us," Fornex said confidently.

I hugged Megan and Fornex and thanked them heartily for their priceless help.

"When you get out of the tunnel," I began, "it will be night, and I want you to look at the brightest star and tell it that you are okay. I will look at the same star and it will bring me the message that you are fine."

Then I left. It was dark outside the passage, but there was a full moon, and it lit the ground. I was very tired from the sleepless night, so I stopped right there and lay under the sky. I looked at my bright star and I thought of my friends who risked their lives to help me. Then I closed my eyes and fell asleep right away. I must have slept for two or three hours, then I woke up and I saw the bright star again. It blinked, as if nodding to tell me that Fornex and Megan were good and safe.

A wave of joy passed through my soul, and I continued peacefully my sweet dream.

The following days, I walked through fields and hilly lands. I stopped to dine with the shepherds, and in the evening I fell asleep, dreaming about that reverie, perhaps imaginary man.

One morning, I was woken by a butterfly on my hand, tickling me. I opened my eyes and saw the beautiful creature with its exquisite blue and purple wings. It flew carefree to the horizon, and my gaze followed it. In the distance, I saw a valley, and after I had breakfast, consisting of some dry bread and honey I had collected a few day ago, I headed for the valley. I walked all day under the hot sun and got really tired. I stopped to rest a little by a well and thought that there should be a village somewhere nearby. I was so tired that I closed my eyes, but the sunrays penetrated through my eyelids and painted strange silhouettes.

I could hear the delicate warble of a small stream flowing somewhere close. Then I felt someone touching my shoulder. I opened my eyes and turned to see who it was. It was like a flash of lightning passed through my whole body, and for a moment, I felt like I would fall to the ground breathless. It was he! I finally found him! He was so handsome, so real. I watched him, and my eyes filled with tears of joy. He asked me if I wanted to dance and didn't wait to hear my answer but grabbed my hand. He led me to the stream and hugged me gently.

I walked to the end of the world to find this man. Stirred to motion by a strange thrill, led by a mysterious power, overthrown and broken, but then uplifted and revived, I reached him. Everything seemed to me as if it was a dream, as if my epic journey led me to a mirage, but here he was next to me, real, touchable, a person of flesh and blood standing beside me and holding my hand.

Flight

The little bird was badly wounded, but she had to keep flying.

The pain wouldn't stop and she fell to the ground. Outside, it was dark and cold. Her wings had become dirty and she felt as if she couldn't move them anymore. There had been better times.

How do birds die? Somehow in secret, somewhere far away. The little bird was living the last minutes of her life, but she wanted to die in one particular place. Although the unbearable pain would lead to her demise, she managed to find strength to continue the flight, her last flight.

A few years ago, a girl took a walk in nice sunny weather in a forest near her home. The sun brightened her face, and her hair fluttered in the soft wind of spring. She wore a silk red gown, which made her look like a beautiful rose. She walked along the creek, on a secret path, which almost no one knew about. She saw the contours of a figure far away, someone was heading in her direction. Only very rarely people used this path, so the girl felt a little uneasy and decided to hide behind a tree, from there she would observe. The figure turned out to be a young man who approached, looking thoughtful. Making a step backwards, the girl cracked a fallen branch, and the young man heard the sound. He looked to the tree and saw a small part of the red gown unobscured. He was curious to see what was behind it and started walking towards the tree, slowly revealing the girl it hid, whose cheeks reddened. For a moment, neither he nor she knew what to say, and the girl felt her heart started to quiver.

"How do you do!" spoke the man, looking at her with great interest. "I didn't know that there are secret paths in this forest where you can find fairies!" They both smiled.

"I come here often but I never saw you before!" said the girl and touched her hair gently.

"I have come here for the first time," said he, "I live elsewhere, far away, but I came here for archery in the forest and decided to have a little walk. Would you like to walk with me?"

"Yes, that would be nice. There is a meadow across the creek full of beautiful flowers. I would show it to you," said the girl with an amiable smile.

This was the beginning of a love story that started like a tiny water spring and developed into an ocean. An indefinable power created a fine thread between the two. They started spending a lot of time together, mostly after tiring day of chores, watching the sunset and taking walks in the darkness of the night. He whispered tender words in her ear, and she felt warm inside being around him. Whenever he held her in his arms, she felt as if that was where she belonged.

She had shown him a little garden not far from the forest where they started reading books together. As he read, the girl was admiring the tone of his voice. Feelings between the two were growing stronger.

Everything between them was beautiful and harmonious, up to the day when the young man suddenly began to change. Their meetings became rarer, the boy said that he was always busy with his archery lessons and duties at home. It so happened that one day he didn't appear on the agreed upon date and didn't let her know why. The girl was hurt. She sensed something had changed, something was wrong and she couldn't find peace. She didn't know what to do with her feelings, which were like clashing waves inside her. At night, she couldn't go to sleep, the hours seemed endless to her. As the first light of dawn appeared on the horizon, she was already dressed and made her way to the forest, taking the same secret path, where they once had met and she saw that he was there. Thoughtful he sat at the riverside. When she saw him, an instant flood of warmth filled her heart; she went nearer to him and embraced him, but he did not answer this gesture of tenderness. Instead, he said that this was the last time he would come to this place and their last encounter. The girl didn't know why he would say something like that and what might be the reason for the change in him. His words penetrated her heart like a dagger.

She asked him why he didn't love her anymore, but he only answered that his path and her path had to split, and that it was of no use to ask questions. And so he left her alone and went away. She fell on her knees, desperately hoping that was just a bad dream. She looked after him and saw the silhouette walking away from her.

In the following months, the girl realised it was not possible for her to stop loving him. And since he wasn't in her life anymore, she had lost her will to live.

She wanted to find a way to leave this world, which felt like a desert to her, so she set off on a journey into the broad world.

Life is meaningless when you've lost your heart, she was thinking.

The girl was wandering far and away, and the road seemed endless.

One day, while walking on a narrow path, an elderly man appeared coming towards her. He saw a tear rolling down her face and falling to the dusty footpath.

"What we wish for, defines our path," said the old man.

The girl wanted to keep walking, but felt that she should listen to what the man had to say.

"Your tear carries a message. The pain you have inside is not letting you live. What would you like to gain?"

She looked in this old man's eyes, eyes full of wisdom and kindness. There was something extraordinary about him, which made her feel as if he possessed something she longed for.

"I want to be with the man whom I carry in my heart, and I want us to love each other like we once did," said the girl, her eyes alight with hope.

"You want to love and to be loved in return. A desire like this oftentimes is unfulfillable when you love a person who is not destined to be yours. Your tears are bitter and they will remain so, that I cannot help you with.

But I have the power to let you see your beloved one once again. I will transform you into a bird and so you will fly and you will see again the one whom you desire.

Your life as a bird will last only three days, and after that, you shall not be in this world anymore."

The old man looked at the girl, feeling her pain. He looked as someone who had experienced all humanly pains. Sorrow was engraved in his face. And now, the girl perceived how noble and at the same time sad looked the old man.

"I wanted to be a tiny little part of the life of whom I love, and that there would be a place for me in his heart. As this is not possible, I wish to become a bird, so I will find a way to be near him. The old man closed his eyes and breathed heavily. And with a soft voice he said: "For love she was born, but love she didn't find. May she go where her heart is!"

The girl felt how the dust from the ground slowly crawled onto her body and covered her entirely. There was strong wind engulfing her from all directions, and when the air became calm once again, before the old man, there was a little bird so beautiful like no one has ever seen before. The old man took her in his hands and spoke, tears brimming: "Fly little bird, fly over the earth and find the one who has wounded your heart. I hope you will find peace."

The little bird flew away. It was a wonderful feeling to spread her wings and to soar in the air.

But after a little while, she felt sharp pain within. She was still far away from her beloved one. The little bird perched on a twig of a weeping willow to take a breath.

"Little bird, why are you so tired?" asked the weeping willow and pulled the twig, on which the bird was resting, closer.

"I fly over the earth seeking the one I love. I am just a little bird who doesn't have enough strength to reach the place of a distant dream."

And the little bird told her story to the old tree.

"You have gone so far all alone, seeking something unreachable. I feel grief for you," said the weeping willow, shuffling her branches, whispering sorrow.

"Even though he is far away, I will find him. My wish was granted by the old man and I have little time left," said the bird.

"They call me a weeping willow, because sadness isn't something distant to me. I understand the hardships of people and all creatures and all the pain, which they experience. But I have never heard a story like yours before. How much pain you must have in your heart little bird! Love is sorrow. I hope you find what you most desire."

"Although the pain I feel is strong, I will reach him and will be in his hands. I shall breathe his essence and shall be near his heart."

The little bird flew and left the weeping willow alone, immersed in silence.

The bird flew high above the clouds, breathing in the smell of rain. She spread her wings, floating in the air, losing sense of time. She was getting closer to the place where her beloved one was, when suddenly she felt sharp pain again, which left her breathless. She started falling to the ground, a drop of blood coming out of her heart. A young man working on the fields beneath noticed the falling bird.

"Are you wounded little bird?" said the young man reaching to take the bird in his hands wanting to heal her wound. She stayed there a brief moment and then leaped into the air and flew again.

What a strange bird, he thought, *I've never seen one so beautiful! I would be glad to treat her wound and then she would be mine.*

The little bird was flying again, drops of blood kept falling down from her heart to the ground.

She had been flying a long time, until she finally reached the little garden, in which she had spent a lot of time with the one she loved. She landed on the bench, where they had often sat. She felt cold and started trembling.

"How I dream he would be here and warm me. How I wish he were here to cure my pain." These thoughts gave her strength.

The night was long and brought about a sickening morning. The little bird hardly found power to fly once more. On the bench remained a trace of blood from the fatally wounded heart.

The young man was near; she felt his presence. The closer she came to him, the less life she had left in her. Then she saw him, only a few steps away. She flew up, and the young man saw her. The bird fell down before his feet. He took her in his hands and wondered what this strange bird was.

Then she looked at him. Her look, the expression of her warm eyes, seemed familiar to him.

Her heart was beating very fast. Although she was transformed into a bird, she was finally in his hands, and there she felt no pain anymore. She was dying. At last, she felt warmth and peace within her soul. She lied down in his tender hands, and her heart stopped beating.

Without knowing, the young man was holding in his hands the girl with whom fate had crossed his path.

He felt sad about the bird which was dying in his hands, but couldn't do anything about it. So he left it on the ground and went on his way.

Very late that evening, the man who saw the bird falling in the field before, was riding his horse.

He glimpsed a rather extraordinary view: a rainbow of bright colours in the far distance, glowing in the dark. He was amazed by this view and decided to ride in this direction. He galloped hard, as if led by some strange invisible force. When he got to the place where the glowing rainbow emerged from, he saw the bird laying there breathless. He walked over to her and took her in his hands, caressing her tiny head gently. Then he saw behind the rainbow a figure of an old man passing by. Then suddenly, the rainbow gathered around the bird's body and lifted her out of his hands into the air. The colourful light grew brighter and brighter, and he saw the bird transforming into a maiden.

The old man smiled through tears and said to the man from the fields:

"You wished to cure the little bird and look after her. Your wish is granted," and vanished into the night.

The love story which ended tragically opened the way for a new one to blossom. The desire of the pure-hearted man from the fields brought life and happiness to a fatally wounded heart. The maiden was revived and joy replaced her sadness. The kind-hearted man enlightened her life and they lived happily ever after.

Utopia

Spring rain had poured over the park. It smelled good, the aroma of the blossoming trees blended in a pleasant fragrance. Amaria was walking through the park on her way back home after work and enjoying her rest, tasting the sweet smell of spring. She was a young woman in her prime. Yet, she had seen the different facets of life, the alternating ebbs and flows.

A little boy, about six years old, walked by her and cast her a curious gaze. Amaria noticed this. Suddenly the silhouettes of the people around her started moving in a great hurry, the world span like a carousel. *What's happening!* she thought confusedly, and looked around, turning in different directions, trying to understand what was going on. She saw only the little boy. He was still standing in the same spot, looking at her with the same strange eyes, as if he knew something. His gaze puzzled her, but not in a frightening way. Amaria closed her eyes for a moment, and when she opened them, the world had stopped spinning. Yet, Amaria wasn't in the park she was just a moment ago. She found herself in a field full of flowers and trees, and completely unfamiliar. She didn't know what to think, a strange sensation swept through her mind. She didn't know whether to stay where she was or go somewhere.

It was quiet and pleasant in the field. A sweet aroma was filling the air, sunlight streaming through the blossoms and leaves, tracing countless little paths among the plants.

Although she didn't know what was going on, Amaria didn't feel in danger. That is why she decided to sit and wait, though she had no idea what she would be waiting for. It hasn't been a long time when she saw a human silhouette in the distance. As the person approached her, Amaria saw it was a man.

"Hello," he said. He was young, her age, and she thought that he looked very handsome.

"Hello," Amaria said, expecting to receive some kind of explanation about the strange circumstances.

"What is your name?" continued the young man, "I am Ader."

"My name is Amaria."

There was a brief silence, only their eyes did the talking. She was looking at him with interest without being ashamed. And he seemed to be barely restraining himself from hugging her.

"You must know more than me, what is this place, and how have I come here?" Amaria broke the silence.

Ader looked at her lips and spoke:

"We're out of reality. This is the only place where we can meet."

"I don't understand, what does that mean – out of reality? And why should we meet as we do not know each other?" Amaria asked.

"We know each other. You are my soul mate, the missing half of me."

Having said that, Ader grabbed her waist, pressed her tightly against his chest and kissing her passionately on the lips.

"You don't know how long I've been waiting for you," he said.

Amaria didn't step away from him. Some strong appeal to this man made her to return his kiss. She thought she hadn't seen him before, otherwise she wouldn't have forgotten him. But what he said sounded like the absolute truth, although illogical. His kiss was so familiar, so pleasant. Amaria didn't know what was going on, but she felt somewhat cosy.

"We don't have much time, Amaria. I know you have a lot of questions, but we don't have enough time for you to understand the answers."

While he was talking, she stared at his eyes. His gaze seemed familiar. Then, in the back of her mind, a short fragment of a long-forgotten past flashed. She was sitting by a river, with her feet immersed in the water, when the same man who was now standing in front of her came to her and wrapped his arms around her in a warm embrace. Then came the memory about the gaze of the little boy, who was looking at her in that peculiar way.

Ader grabbed her hand and kissed her again, as if he couldn't get enough of her. And she was still silent, not understanding.

"Your gaze... It's so familiar, I've seen you before by that river... and the eyes of that little boy..." she said puzzled.

"Yes, it was me. We met each other in reality. So... it seems I was a child this time. Amaria, I know you don't remember, but we've known each other for a long time. Time does not exist here, this place is beyond reality. That is why we can only meet here. Now I am yours and you are mine. There are no boundaries and obstacles, no age or distance. Only you and me." At these words, tears appeared in his eyes, "You do not know how long I've been waiting for you."

Ader smiled, knowing that he couldn't know exactly for how long, because time didn't exist here.

Amaria took in every word, every gaze of Ader.

"You say we know each other, but how is this possible? When did we meet?"

"Just remember that I love you. I love you so much... Amaria... "

At that moment, everything started spinning around again and Ader vanished. The sunny field and the pleasant scent disappeared. Amaria couldn't apprehend what was going on. And in the next moment, everything around her was static. Buildings, people. She walked forward and looked at her image in a window she was passing by. The sight struck her, she was no longer a young woman, but a girl, perhaps at age 12. Then she heard a baby crying from somewhere. She looked up and saw a young woman embracing a tiny being – a just born baby. Her heart raced.

"Nymra, what are you doing, stop getting distracted," a female voice interrupted, and a tall woman came to her and held her by the arm, "Come on, let's go home."

It was her mother. Nymra recalled everything. She was twelve, clearly remembering her childhood, her school, her friends. But she also remembered herself as a young woman. She remembered the park, the boy and Ader. She remembered the sunny garden.

Several years passed. Nymra was now nineteen years old. She often went to the park where the mother was walking her son, and she saw him. The boy had Ader's eyes. He was looking at her with the same eyes, curious, but not understanding. Nymra knew it was him. And then the same inexplicable thing happened, everything started spinning around again and she found herself in the sunny field.

"Ader, where are you?" She shouted desperately. But there was no one. She fell to the ground and wept helplessly. Then the night fell, as warm as the day. The moonlight gently caressed the flowers. And she waited for Ader.

Not long after, he appeared. He stopped a step away from her and said nothing, just looked in her eyes and hugged her. Amaria started crying.

"Do not cry, my dear, I'm here now."

The two stayed this way, sad, but at the same time happy that they are together in this moment. They had so much to say, but didn't know when they would have to go back to reality.

"You know, I was there when you were born," Amaria smiled, "I watched you grow up. In reality your name was Marco."

Ader also smiled.

"And this time, what was your name?" he asked.

"Nymra," she told him.

The two met secretly from the world. Sometimes, they did not say a word and just looked at each other. Sometimes, she was crying, and he comforted her. Sometimes, he could not stand it anymore, and she hugged him gently. Their love was utopia. Reality condemned them to loneliness.

They also met in reality. A little girl met an elderly man, they smiled at each other and moved forward. A middle-aged woman passed by a little boy, looked at him for a moment and continued her way. That was their predestined fate, years separated them forever. There was nothing they could do to change that and to be together.

The only place where their love was possible was beyond reality.

Life is an inscrutable thread. A place for meetings and a place to pass each other, weaving with crossroads, where time is an obstacle as elusive as the stars upon it sits.

The Two Leaves

Every morning the sun warmed the frozen branches of the old tree and helped it gather strength for the rest of the cold winter. The tree had lived through so many years. It knew all the whims of the seasons and had become very wise.

And so, this winter was almost over. The darkness of the night gave way to the gentle morning sun.

The tree awoke from its dream and gladly welcomed the arrival of the warm wind. Spring was here!

As always, the snowdrops were the most impatient flowers and the first to show. After them, the crocuses, the tulips and the hyacinths joyfully looked at the world. The colourful irises, primrose and violets soon joined them. Everyone considered the shy lily-of-the-valley, which blossoms always looked down, as the most gentle and frail. The branches of the old tree were also sprinkled with hundreds of tiny blossoms, and they were the most fragrant. The whole land had become a flower garden.

A little leaf appeared on one of the branches. It had barely shown itself when another one sprang next to it. Both small and light green leaves grew up together and showed their faces to the world.

How beautiful spring was! A source of life and glowing joy. A harbinger to the hot summer. The two leaves rejoiced in the sun, and the flowers smiled sweetly at them.

As summer arrived, the two leaves grew bigger and stronger. Still, one of them was thinner and more fragile, and the other was thicker and more robust. The bigger leaf looked at the smaller one and said,

"You know, I really wanted to tell you something. In the beginning of the spring when we were growing up together, I thought how pleasant it was to be near you."

The smaller leaf smiled shyly and said,

"I like being in your company, too."

The two green leaves became very close. They talked every day. The wind playfully passed them by and made them swing. They danced in the air, under the sound of the birds' songs.

When it was raining, it felt so joyous! They drank eagerly from the water that gave them life.

One night, however, something unusual happened. Instead of rain, from the sky fell hail that could hurt the leaves. The stronger leaf then stretched its edges to the more fragile, which trembled with fear. The night was long and dark and the little leaf was trembling, but it felt protected.

In the morning, the bigger leaf had a few scars from the large grains that fell on it.

"Didn't it hurt when you leaned over me to protect me?" the delicate leaf asked. The bigger one looked at it with affection and replied courageously:

"Do you want me to always stretch my tips over you and keep you from harm?"

Yes, they were in love. Two small green leaves among so many others like them. They were meant to be born near each other and to love one another. Everything was beautiful and gentle. At the height of summer, small berries were born around them, and everyone was very happy.

The summer sun was hiding behind the horizon. The sunset was so beautiful, everything was dipped in red, and clouds were drawing strange paintings with different shades of pink. The two leaves had already lost their juicy and deep green colour and slowly turned orange. The landscape has changed everywhere. There were no small flowers, and the grass was yellow. Hard-working animals collected food for the winter.

The old tree knew it would soon have to part with its children – this year's leaves. It was hard for it to watch the circle of life every year. Each season it was the same – small green leaves were born only to fall down from its branches before the winter comes.

Autumn leaves fell from the tree and covered the ground with a soft, colourful carpet. The two, now old, leaves tore away from the tree and fled smoothly to the ground. It was their last dance, and they were flying in the cold starry night. They fell side by side, touching at the edges. Together, they would sink into the dust and merge into one.

Reality

They were born in a world of high technology. Science had reached unexpected heights, people lived most comfortably, with splendid amenities and special technologies that made life easy and enjoyable.

Although technology had developed so much, the society was the same as millennia ago. People were driven by the same interests – desire for success, for power and money.

But modern world had succeeded in aggravating selfishness and trampling the remnants of virtue in people. There was no sense of empathy or integrity in people, instead intrigues were created and unfair games were played.

Two human souls had appeared in this world, determined not to live according the laws of modern times. Would they also be broken by reality? Would their light be extinguished before it had gathered the power to ignite?

At first glance, Karaman was an ordinary youth, no different from the others. He was well educated, pleasant in appearance, polite, but very secretive. No one was able to look into his mind and reveal what kind of person he was. Karaman liked to observe people and analyse society and didn't allow anyone to control him. He was a student, from a good family and had a promising future.

His father Rizzo was a rich man. With his parents' inheritance and his sharp sense for profitable deals, he had multiplied his money in a remarkable way, and then entered politics. Here he was able to exercise his greatest talent – to manipulate. He liked to command, and as a politician, he had the opportunity to use his abilities not just over a small group of people but also over whole societies.

Having managed to remain completely in the shadow of his father all the years of his life, Karaman was not popular. He was expected to become a great man and successful politician one day, but until then he had a peaceful life.

His meeting with Agapia happened on a cold winter day, when everything outside was covered with frost. Karaman was in Mavros Square, waiting for his fellow students to gather and go for a warm cup of tea. He had come fifteen minutes early and stood with his hands in his pockets, staring in the distance with an impassive look, as if the cold didn't affect him. At that time, a young girl passed him by. When Karaman looked at her, a hidden string in his heart trembled. One wouldn't say that the girl was stunningly beautiful, but Karaman felt attracted to her since the first moment he saw her. She also looked at him and then went away. Her gaze was determined, but kind and gentle.

Karaman wanted to go over to her but didn't have courage. He somehow felt he would see her again.

Karaman went to the same square at the same time a month later. It was still freezing cold and there weren't many people outside. Agapia stood waiting for someone, and Karaman walked past her. They met each other's gaze and Karaman felt the same hidden string in his soul.

At that time came an elderly man with glasses, intelligent look on his face and dignified posture. He was the person Agapia was waiting for.

Karaman changed the direction he was walking in and went into the coffee shop next to the square, and in just few moments, the girl and the elderly gentleman came in too.

Their conversation seemed to be important, judging by the emotions that showed on the girl's face. Her eyebrows creased and painted an unusual expression of pain.

The next morning, Karaman got up and went to Mavros Square. He saw the same girl sitting on a bench, watching the wind playing with the snowflakes falling on the ground, swirling them into an elegant dance.

Karaman sad beside her and looked at her. She looked back and gave him a faint smile. After a few silent moments, she was the first to speak.

"Do you think it's possible to change the reality?"

"I think it is possible to change the reality, unless you allow the reality to change you," answered Karaman.

On this cold winter day, two small flames lit up. Karaman and Agapia found companionship and warmth in each other. They had the same ideas about the world and wanted to make a change.

Meanwhile, his father was playing his political games on a large scale. He didn't care about anyone and he didn't stop at anything. For years, he had been working on a project for eradicating dependence on natural resources. His aim was to replace the main sources of food and life with artificial ones and to build an entire empire based on that. Clear cutting of forests had begun decades earlier, and he wanted to remove them completely. With the power of technology, he said, people would no longer need them.

The elderly gentleman Agapia was talking to on that day in the coffee shop was a professor protecting the existence of ecosystems. Agapia was his right hand. She never showed herself openly, but she acted behind the scenes sabotaging Rizzo's power. He knew this very well and was trying to destroy her and the professor.

First, he had her thrown out of university. Then she lost her job at the research centre, and now he targeted the professor, the only person who was close to Agapia, and who was the only family to her.

When Karaman became aware of all this, he began to furiously resist his father's plans, but wasn't successful. The father-son conflict became so fierce that Rizzo drove him out of the house. He knew that while Agapia was close to his son, he would not be able to turn Karaman into a copy of himself. So, he was looking for a way to crush her down once and for all.

Agapia and Karaman were very different from other people, and could never fully fit in the society. They faced the problems together and although they couldn't change the way things worked, they weren't giving up. Their love grew bigger and bigger, and turned into a blazing fire. They could not live without each other and were inseparable.

Their strong relationship exasperated Rizzo, who kept on searching of ways to separate them.

One of his scientists had invented a machine, which finally gave Rizzo the solution to how to make his son obey him. In just one day, he would change both of their fates, using modern technology of influencing the human brain to erase their memory.

On one cloudy day, when Agapia was going to the professor's house, she noticed two men in grey suits walking behind her. She felt she should hide from them and quickened her step. She went down a narrow street and hid behind the corner of a building. She waited there for a few minutes, holding her breath. When she walked out of the street, there was no one behind her. She took a breath and hurried on her way. A moment later, the two pursuers showed up in front of her. She turned around and started running. But they outran her, grabbed her, squeezed her in their car and took her to the clinic sponsored by Rizzo. When they pushed her into one of the rooms where the light was so strong that she could barely keep her eyes open, she saw that Karaman was there too. He came to her and hugged her tightly. A tear rolled down his cheeks when he kissed her.

The machine was there, in this isolated room, locked from outside. They knew what this machine was created for. Their memory would be wiped off and they wouldn't remember anything about each other. There was nothing they could do, no way to escape from here.

Their eyes met perhaps for the last time. Cold sweat wetted Karaman's forehead. Their hearts were beating fast, and a sense of fear overwhelmed them. A huge resentment and anger struggled in Karaman. But there was nothing to be done. Agapia's eyes stared at him with pain, and in his, she could see love, and a promise. A promise that he will never forget her.

Then they were forced to sit in special chairs, and for hours, the cell waves erased their memories for the past years one by one.

Rizzo was satisfied. He had already prepared a brilliant future for his son, he pictured him as a great politician and a public figure.

He had taken care of Agapia. Instead of killing her, he decided to send her away from his son and never let her appear before him. At the other end of the world, she would begin her new life. She would stay with a family she didn't know, and they would tell her that soon after she lost her parents, she lost her memory too.

Several years passed after the cellular radiation. Karaman has recently come to the political scene under the patronage of his father. But unlike him, he didn't want to manipulate people and found it very hard to work on the project for replacing the natural sources with artificial ones. One day during a conference where he had to do the speech, he stood in front of the crowd and started reading the script: "Dear citizens, we have gathered together to celebrate control over nature instead of being controlled by nature."

He stopped in this moment. A shadow of a thought crossed his mind as if there was something he had to say, but it slipped his mind. People from the audience started to whisper at one another about this strange man.

Rizzo was on the first row and came to the stage, continuing the speech.

All these years he and Agapia felt they had forgotten something, but no matter how hard they tried, they could not remember what. That made them feel some kind of a void in their lives, and they were unhappy.

During cold winters' days, they felt some strange inner warmth, as if some faded forgotten picture had popped in their minds, but they could not remember anything specific about it.

Often Karaman woke up, covered in sweat. That night, he had a dream. He had seen two eyes, the eyes of a woman, so strangely familiar, so close. Since that night, he started searching for them in reality. Walking down the streets, Karaman was trying to get a hold on those eyes, to meet that gaze. He was looking for them everywhere, but could not find them.

At the other end of the world, Agapia was suffocating, leading a life that wasn't hers. She was getting up early and walking around for hours, trying to overcome the sense of loss she was feeling.

One day, she went to the train station and bought a ticket for a random destination. She was caring only a small suitcase, not knowing where she was going. Perhaps she will somehow find the missing part of her, she thought. Agapia kept travelling far and away.

Months passed one by one, leaving painful traces. Once Karaman was sitting on the bench in Mavros Square. A woman passed him by, walking slowly. She was looking down at the little snowflakes that the wind was twirling at her feet. Karaman got up. The woman stopped and turned around. He went to her and took her cold hand. He finally found the eyes from his dream.

"I found you. It is you, it has always been you" Karaman said through tears.

Agapia felt as if her heart will burst of excitement. She hasn't felt so alive before this moment, when he was there, in front of her, holding her hand. And her eyes filled with tears of joy.

"Do you think our life is a part of reality?" she asked.

"Only if we allow reality to swallow us," replied Karaman."

They remembered every detail of their lost lives. All the wasted years vanished in a moment. They saw only hope and their shared future ahead of them. And they never split up again.

Reality did not succeed in crushing them. Instead, Agapia and Karaman created their own reality.

The Soundless Violin

In the house of an old music teacher, there was a very distinguished violin. It was made of wood from a tree, which had lived for a long time. Under this tree, many people's paths had crossed and separated over the years. The tree had seen good and bad, had experienced sunny days and cold winters. But the most precious thing, which the tree could observe throughout its whole life, was love. Love of the birds feeding their offspring, love of the cuddly squirrels, hopping from its branches playfully chasing each other. Love of a young man and woman, born in the same year, who met under the old tree. The tree had seen their entire life and had witnessed the harmony between them. Their true love was remembered by the tree and engraved deep into his trunk.

When the old tree was cut down, its wood was used to make beautiful pieces of furniture. Each home, where a piece of that furniture was placed, was full of happiness and harmony as the old tree brought warmth to the people living there. Little wooden figures of the old tree made children happy. They were more eager to play with them than with any other toys.

But the most noteworthy creation which was made out of the old tree, was a mysterious violin. When it was finished, whoever tried to play it had no success, for the violin did not want to give out its sound. An old music teacher had bought the violin years ago, and sometimes he gave it to his students, so that they could try and make the violin sing, but the violin remained silent.

One morning, at quarter to eight, there was a knock on the door of the old music teacher.

It was a new student – a handsome young man. His lively character and good manners made him the teacher's favourite student. He practised with great energy and put a lot of feeling into the music he played. The teacher saw his passion, and so once, he decided to present to him the beautiful violin.

"Nobody until this day has played on this violin my lad," said the teacher with a mysterious note in his voice, "Try and see if you can make it sing."

The young man thanked his teacher and eagerly took the violin from his hands. The old man smiled and left his student alone in the room.

The boy looked at the beautiful instrument and touched its surface tenderly. He placed it on his shoulder and how surprised he was, when there was no sound coming out of the exquisite instrument. He was trying again and again, but the violin didn't want to make a sound.

When his teacher came back, the young man asked him what kind of magic is upon this violin so that it doesn't want to make a sound. The teacher tapped him on the shoulder and said perhaps he should practise a little more and try again another time.

The student put even more effort and passion into his practice and began to compose music of his own. One of his works, he devoted to the mysterious violin, and into this melody, he had put his true feelings from his heart. And when he next went to his teacher, he asked him to play the mysterious violin once again.

The old man agreed and brought him the violin. Again, he left the room so that the young man could practise undisturbed.

His beautiful hands caressed the violin and its strings. He set it at his shoulder and spoke the words: "Oh magical violin, play and let me hear the sounds, which I have composed inspired by you," and he played a beautiful melody. And now the violin began to play so wonderful as no other violin ever had played. Every string sang joyfully when the fingers of the young musician touched them. He played with his eyes shut and his heart open. The old teacher entered, astonished by the music, which made even passers-by stop and listen, overwhelmed.

"No doubt, the violin likes you young man!" he said excitedly, "Never before have I heard music so beautiful!"

The next day, the old teacher decided to give the violin to some of his other students, but in their hands, the violin was soundless. Even the teacher himself tried to play, he chose a beautiful melody to play on it and touched the strings with the bow. But the violin remained silent. It seemed to only want to sing in the hands of the young man.

The violin had fallen in love with him. For this reason, it didn't give out any sound when someone else touched it. It was able to let go only in his hands and didn't want anyone else to play it.

Few years passed by since the young student of music had touched the mysterious violin for the first time. The old teacher made him a very special present, the only asset the young man needed to play and produce beautiful music to make people happy, his favourite magic violin. He became a successful musician who was loved by his audience. He performed all over the world, with the mysterious violin in his hands.

The years slipped by like the little grains of sand in an hourglass. The talented musician grew old and his grey hair evoked reverence. He held the violin for the last time. Though his hands were not as fast as they used to be, the violin sang as beautifully as always, in the hands of her beloved musician. The music he played touched people's hearts and brought warmth and peace to them. They would always remember the wonderful feeling the mysterious violin had left in their soul.